Thus a Kiss

CJ Love

Mysteries by CJ Love

VERONA'S VINEYARD COZY MYSTERIES SERIES
Juliet & Dead Romeo
O' Happy Dagger
Thus With a Kiss
Stage of Fools

Romantic Comedy by CJ Love
Lucy Goes Wilde
Wilde at Heart
Wilde Card

Historical Romance by CJ Love
For the Love of Murphy
For the Love of Lauralee
For the Love of Eileen (coming soon)

Thus With a Kiss

Verona's Vineyard Cozy Mysteries, Book 3

CJ Love

Secret Staircase Books

Thus With a Kiss
Published by Secret Staircase Books, an imprint of
Columbine Publishing Group, LLC
PO Box 416, Angel Fire, NM 87710

Book layout and design by Secret Staircase Books
Cover design by Cynthia Whitten-Love

First trade paperback edition: June, 2020
First e-book edition: June, 2020

* * *

Publisher's Cataloging-in-Publication Data

Love, CJ
Thus With a Kiss / by CJ Love.
p. cm.
ISBN 978-1649140067 (paperback)
ISBN 978-1649140074- (e-book)

1. Juliet Da Vinci (Fictitious character)—Fiction. 2. Shakespearean
themes—Fiction. 3. Women sleuths—Fiction. I. Title

Verona's Vineyard Cozy Mystery Series : Book 3.
Love, CJ, Verona's Vineyard cozy mysteries.

BISAC : FICTION / Mystery & Detective.

813/.54

For Thea Tova Busby, who's brought such joy into all of our lives.

"I will kiss thy lips."

Chapter 1

The Blonde Palace.

That's what Juliet Da Vinci called the mega-mansion she visited, on occasion, with her mother. The Novak family who owned the place were all blonde-headed, some even naturally so.

The mansion stood on hundreds of acres of land bordering Lake Erie. The Novaks had christened the residence Vyšehrad, after ancient ruins in a Czechia city from where the family hailed. Prague, perhaps.

Somewhere over there.

Juliet Da Vinci was not well versed in geography—

except Italy and New York. Sure, she'd traveled to foreign lands in her twenty-four years of life. But who needed to fly to Czechia when her mother's new best friend, Saskia Novak, lived in a domed castle complete with a replica of the Charles Bridge?

Juliet had spent the day at Vyšehrad preparing for the evening event: The Valentine's Day Ball. Everyone on the guest list arrived between eleven and one o'clock because Saskia had hired The Great Gatsby's movie designer to outfit everyone. Assistants performed tailoring on the spot.

Downstairs, the enormous reception hall comfortably accommodated the two hundred guests who'd gathered for the party. A thousand potted lemon trees formed a maze to the dining area, and tucked here and there were seating areas with lamp lighting. That was where Juliet walked with Paris Nobleman.

Paris wore a white tuxedo well suited to his slender frame and broad shoulders. His nearly black hair was waxed and lifted off his head like a tsunami, which highlighted his green eyes and angular features.

"Have I told you that you look beautiful in that dress, Miss Daisy?"

"Yes, you have." Turning her face, Juliet pretended coy and batted her lashes. She wore a gold lame underdress with a two-inch crystal teardrop accented sheath that tied at the waist. One of the hairstylists had tamed her wild curls with a band of satin. They'd used water wax on her front tendril to form a curl on her forehead. "I don't think I'm supposed to be Daisy. I'm sure Mali or Jana have claimed that character."

Paris stopped in front of her and reached forward, touching a teardrop at Juliet's waist. "They don't look half as good as you do, yeah?"

Juliet watched his fingers rub the teardrop for a moment. "The costume lady went all out, didn't she? And you," she said, catching his eyes. "You look like Jay Gatsby in your white tuxedo."

Paris dropped his hand, his eyes falling to the jacket's lapel. "I asked for anything but white."

"I never liked the movie. It was about a bunch of awful flappers and gangsters who cheated on each other and drank Gin Rickeys."

He tilted his head. "Yet, you personify the unattainable Daisy."

"Unattainable? I've begged you to come to Italy with my family tomorrow, and you refuse me. You are the one who's playing hard to get."

"Italy? Pfft. All medieval and enchanting."

"Matera is wonderful. You'd love it: little restaurants in alleyways, flower boxes on every window, and the beach…" she inhaled, "… is gorgeous."

With hooded eyes, he took a step nearer. "No one speaks English."

"I'll be your interpreter," she told him, not retreating.

"No indoor plumbing, and you have to walk everywhere."

"We're not visiting the eighteen hundreds, Paris. My cousin lives in a villa at the top of the mountain and owns a car."

"No thanks," he said, his hands landing on her waist. "I have responsibilities here."

"You keep saying that." Her hands landed on his forearms. "What responsibilities?"

"I'll tell you when you get home from Italy." Pressing

his fingers into her waist, Paris pulled her closer. He'd been growing bolder and bolder recently. His fingers loosened, but then his arm went around and pulled her hard against his chest. Before Juliet objected, his mouth covered hers. His lips were possessive, and playful too, meaning to tease her into loving him.

Juliet's blood warmed and then raced like wildfire through her veins. Then, she pushed him away and scolded, "Paris!"

He leaned away with his eyes wide and his mouth parted, as though he was stunned at his behavior. "How did that happen? You really ought to stop falling into me like that."

She forced down a smile. "You need to stop."

"I won't," he said, his eyes as green as the tree leaves all around them. "You'll be gone for six weeks, yeah? I want you to remember me."

"I'm not that forgetful," she told him, angling away before he kissed her again.

His lips caught her cheek and then moved to her throat.

Juliet didn't push him away.

The sound of high heels clicking on the marble floor came through the trees.

Paris dropped his hands to his sides.

It was an unnecessary maneuver since Juliet's mother was the one to emerge from the lemon trees. Italia would faint from joy if she found Juliet and Paris making out in the bushes.

Saskia Novak followed Italia.

Paris nodded to the ladies and told Juliet, "I'll see you at the table."

Both women wore low-waisted slip gowns. If this were

a beauty pageant, Italia would win the crown. Her dark hair was piled high on her head and with a net of diamonds holding it in place. She wore silver sequins and fringe to her knees, showing off her legs.

Reaching for her, Italia took Juliet's wrists and held them out to her sides. "Don't you look pretty?" She spun Juliet in a half circle. "You should wear your hair like that more often."

"Like a flapper?"

"Oh, you know what I mean," her mother said, dropping Juliet's wrists.

"No," she answered, her hands bouncing off her hips. "No, I don't."

Italia lifted her hand and then brushed Juliet's hair with the back of it. "Be a new you, mix it up once in a while."

Her mother had been doing that a lot lately, wanting a change in her life, wanting to mimic her new bestie, Saskia.

"I like the modern me," Juliet told her.

Saskia lifted her nose and said, "*Vševnálek.*"

What was that? Shezna…?

Saskia was as tall as Italia, but broader and almost masculine in some ways. It was her square and muscular shoulders, perhaps, and a straight waist that filled out the A-line of her dress. Her white-blonde hair was as big as a balloon, slick in the front and coiffed in the round behind her head.

"We went to a lot of expense for you to look so good, Juliet," Saskia told her, pointing her champagne glass at the same time.

"And I thank you," she told her with a small curtsy. "So does Redken hair products. You must've bought it by the vat."

The woman nodded, her halo hair unmoving. "Yes, that and champagne. We've brought in three thousand bottles for tonight, so drink up."

"I've already had a glass," Juliet told her. "It's very pink. And the pearls at the bottom of the glass, are they real?"

Saskia forced a smile. The bottom of her face was blocky, and yet, puffy-cheeked at the same time. Her little mouth pursed. "What do you think?"

I think they are real.

"Where is Hugo?" Italia asked. This was also something new for Italia, attempting a love match between Juliet and Hugo Novak.

"I haven't seen him," she said, her eyes glancing toward the dining area.

"He can't wait to see you," Saskia said, stepping around Juliet and heading toward one of the many staircases. The way she'd said it didn't sound as though Hugo was in a rush to see Juliet. But, then again, Saskia just spoke in that manner, weary and disinterested.

"I can't wait to see him either," she told their retreating backsides. And, she'd meant it too. Juliet loved Hugo, just not like that, and especially with the lingering pressure of Paris' lips on her throat and cheek.

I'm not in love with Paris!

Juliet followed the potted tree trail to the ballroom. She needed to stop Paris' advances – even though his kisses were, well, breathtaking.

Right.

Six weeks away in Matera ought to clear her head a little and settle all the butterflies in her belly. So, in that way, it was a good thing Paris wasn't boarding the flight to Italy in the morning.

Right.

The maze opened up to the dining area. Black tablecloths covered ten-foot round tables with centerpieces made of white ostrich feathers. String lights dangled from the four storied ceiling. Across a large dance floor was a stage where Michael Bublé performed *My Funny Valentine*, and *I Get a Kick Out of You*.

Yes, Michael Bublé, in person, with a sixteen-piece Baroque orchestra accompanying him.

Behind the band were multiple sets of French doors, and outside of the doors, large snowflakes fell. Whoever ordered the natural occurrence ought to be awarded 'Party Planner of the Year' for the added ambiance it brought to the ball.

"There you are," someone said behind Juliet.

It was Emma Moretti standing with her sister, Olive. Of course, they'd attend the ball. The twins were on all social calendars of the giga-rich.

Emma wore sequins and tulle. A stylist had coiffed her lavender hair into a side part and a fringy-in-front-of-the-ear look. She wore a headband, too, pale pink and feathered.

Olive was a much more physically fit woman, preferring golf shorts to dresses, and the designer attired her in a yellow tuxedo and wingtip oxfords in beige and gold. Her shoulder-length hair was auburn and it brought out the blue in her hazel eyes.

"I love the Novak parties," she said, holding up her glass of champagne. "Real pearls!"

"You'll have to remember to do that at your next party," Juliet told her.

Olive shook her head and lowered her fluted glass. "This

party would wipe out my allowance and my inheritance."

Emma took Juliet's arm and faced the stage. Her scent was of the sea, like bursting bubbles of salt and coconut. "I do love Michael Bublé."

Olive took Juliet's other arm. "I hear they flew him in by helicopter."

Her sister leaned forward. "You're such a fangirl." She turned to Juliet–she was close up–and explained, "And I don't mean Bublé. Olive is in line to be Mali Novak's new best friend."

"What?" Juliet leaned away. It was just such an odd idea that Olive and Mali would consider a close friendship at all, as they were such vastly different personalities. Juliet asked, "What happened to the old best friend?"

Olive took over the story. "Taylor lost her status by sleeping with Mali's boyfriend." She released Juliet's arm and faced her. "She still has Teagan at her side, but you know how Mali always keeps two friends at the ready."

Juliet didn't know that at all because she never kept track of the Novaks. That was her mother's pastime. "Since when do you care whether you're best friends with anyone?"

Olive shrugged and the shoulders of her yellow jacket moved stiffly. "Mali is exciting. She's invited me to their family camping trip to Colorado."

Emma leaned forward again, "You mean their luxury chalet in Aspen?" She caught Juliet's eyes. "Mali wants Olive to help her search for aliens while they're out there."

"Oh," Juliet teased, bumping Olive's shoulder with her own. "That is exciting."

Something black moved into her peripheral vision, and Juliet turned toward the dance floor.

There was Hugo Novak in a flocked velvet blazer with satin lapels, black slacks, and black vest. His slicked-back blonde hair revealed a pockmark near his hairline. Hugo's face shape was the same as his mother Saskia's, square with the blocky chin, and with small round lips. He held out his hand toward Juliet and, with a pop of drama, said, "Dance with me!"

"Oh, Hugo," Emma said, laughing. "You look amazing."

He whipped his head around. "Leave me alone, she-cat. I only have eyes for Juliet. Mostly, because Seržant Matka said so."

Juliet asked, "Who is sore-gant matka?"

"My sergeant-mother."

"Breakaway, Hugo, breakaway," Olive advised, grabbing another champagne flute from a passing waiter's plate.

And he did, by pulling Juliet onto the dance floor. He was smooth, barely lifting his feet as he moved to the rhythm of the music.

He was almost as good a dancer as Paris.

Get a grip. You don't love Paris.

Juliet concentrated on Hugo. They danced a single time swing to the lively *I Get a Kick Out of You.*

Hugo twirled her, pushed her to arm's length, and brought Juliet back into a light embrace.

The song ended, and the next began: *The Way You Look Tonight.*

Foxtrot.

Juliet hated foxtrot.

With the slower tempo, she asked, "Is this velvet?" She brushed his shoulder with the tips of her fingers. "Oh, it is. You look good in velvet."

"Tell that to the welts breaking out on my thighs," Hugo said, continuing to lead. "You're better looking than the last girl my mother tried to set me up with." Swinging Juliet around, he added, "Natalie wasn't that cute, to be honest."

"Don't say that."

He shook his head, eyes popping. "How dare you judge me, woman. You didn't see Natalie. You don't know what I had to go through."

Juliet lifted her face and laughed.

A long lens camera came between them.

Hugo jolted to a stop.

Juliet dropped her hands to her side and took a step backward.

On the other end of the camera stood Mali Novak. She was just as blonde as her brother, but with golden and brown highlights naturally twisting throughout her hair. Mali was the same height as Juliet, though she was much curvier, especially in the hips and derriere. It was as though she'd injected Fix-a-Flat back there and pump-pump-pumped it up.

It looks good.

Mali gave Juliet a brief nod and asked her brother, "Have you seen Noah?"

Hugo pushed the camera lens away from his chin with the side of his hand. "I haven't seen him." He winked at Juliet. "Clothed."

Juliet snorted a laugh, shot Mali a look, and then pinched her lips together.

Mali didn't see the humor and stormed off in the direction of the lemon trees again. Her butt rolled around like two big tennis balls caught in a plastic bag.

Hugo reached for Juliet and swung her back onto the floor. Michael Bublé had left the stage, but the orchestra played on.

This time they danced a slow cha-cha. Juliet asked, "Who's Noah?"

"Oh!" Hugo gushed, spinning her and then dipping her. "Let me fill you in on all the scandaliciousness." He kept her in a dip and nodded toward the lemon trees. "Look, over there."

Juliet glanced left. Yes, a gentleman was standing there, but with her head upside down, she didn't see him well.

"That is Noah York." Hugo jerked her upward again, and then cha-cha-cha'd toward the stage. "Jana is such a simple girl, and he'll break her heart. It's only a matter of time." He swung Juliet around full circle. "Oh! See how he's pulled her into the trees? He's calling it all off right now."

"Jana?" Juliet glanced toward the trees again. She hadn't seen Jana. "Call it off? Are they engaged?"

"No, they'll never be engaged. Noah has his diddley in every woman around here."

"Did…?"

"Diddley, diddley," he said, waving one hand. "You know, he's sleeping with everyone."

"Oh… well, what's Noah doing here?"

"Xenia brought him home, like a little pet doggy."

Juliet didn't know Xenia Novak well. She only knew that the older woman was Cyril Novak's sister and that she lived somewhere in the mansion.

Hugo twirled her again. "She found him on one of her adventures, crossing a desert, or climbing up the side of a volcano."

He'd spun her fast, and when she came back around, Juliet clutched Hugo's shoulder hard. "Is that a usual occurrence, bringing someone home?"

"We all have our pets," he said, and then took a long breath through his broad nose. "The problem with Noah is that one of his many women followed him here. Bexley someone or other. She swears she's had Noah's baby."

"Wow."

He nodded, just warming up his gossipy tongue. "Mommy Dearest put an end to the rumor."

The music ended, and Hugo's hand pressed Juliet's back, ushering her toward the dining area. "She made Noah take a paternity test. If he wanted to stay in our home, he had to take the test."

Juliet halted and eyed Hugo. "What happened?"

"The baby is not Noah's child, buuuuuut, I'm sure he slept with the Bexley creature. Why else would she stalk him? And now she's stalking Jana too."

"Because she's dating Noah?"

"Right." He flicked his wrist toward the dining tables. "Look, Mother's watching."

Before Juliet turned around, Hugo planted a sloppy kiss on her mouth. It felt like a wet sponge slapping her on the lips.

It was no Paris Nobleman kiss.

Juliet pulled away from Hugo and brushed her fingers across her mouth. "Why don't you just tell your mom that you're gay?"

"And lose my inheritance, are you mad?" Hugo took her hand. "Will you marry me?" He leaned in further and said, hush-hush, "We can never, you know, consummate the marriage, but we'd have fun, and you'd be filthy rich."

Juliet pulled her hands from Hugo's. "I'm a little more traditional than that."

He blinked and gave a quick shake of his head. "What's more traditional than marrying for money?"

Juliet stepped around him and made her way toward her family's table.

Of all the idiot suggestions…

"If you want a baby, we can make one in a petri dish," Hugo said over her shoulder.

Juliet winced and spun around to face him. "No, Hugo. I won't marry you."

"Fine." Straightening his velvet-covered shoulders, he pouted, "I'll go drown my sorrows in champagne."

Juliet turned toward her family's table, skirted around chairs, and then slipped into her seat. On the right side of her elegant black and gold name card was Italia's. On her left was Hugo's and then Paris'.

Paris strolled to the table, switched cards with Hugo, and sat next to Juliet.

Juliet's father, Santos Da Vinci, came to the table. He wore a pinstripe suit, and what was that, a plaid vest?

Oh, she knew how he hated that. Her father wasn't a plaid anything sort of man. Tweed, yes, expensive shirts, all day long, but plaid? Not on your nelly.

Santos' assigned seat was next to Cyril Novak. Flipping his black cloth napkin, Santos arranged it in his lap.

"This is a nice setup, *sì*?" he said, nodding his salt and pepper hair.

Cyril Novak was a younger man in his late forties, perhaps, and he wore his white-blonde hair parted on the side and swept over his brow. It was possibly a hairpiece, which was confusing. A billionaire should be able to afford hair plugs, at least scalp injections, but Cyril's piece looked like he'd bought it online from a carpet store. It was the shag rug style that needed a wooden rake to straighten it. "Stay a couple of days," he said, motioning to Santos. "I've put in vines."

"What vines? What do you mean, you put in vines?"

Cyril's back hit the chair. "I'm starting a vineyard."

Santos gazed at Juliet while jabbing his thumb in Cyril's direction. "This guy." To Cyril, he asked, "What do you know about vineyards?"

"Nothing," he said in a jovial tone. "That's why I need you. I want a vineyard, the real thing, the rows of vines, and the grapes. I want to make wine." He dropped his hands and laid his forearm on the table. "I've made apple wine, but I want the chardonnay and sauvignon. You're the guy to help me."

Cucumber-avocado soup arrived, served by an army of men and women in black tuxedos.

Hugo came, took his soup bowl, and moved to another table. He was still miffed at Juliet, apparently.

Saskia and Italia sat too, and the vineyard conversation mingled with the tinkling of glasses and cutlery hitting china.

It was during the amuse-bouche course that Paris leaned toward Juliet. "I saw Hugo kiss you."

Juliet lifted her napkin and dabbed her mouth. "He asked me to marry him."

Paris' green eyes drifted off for a moment and then snapped back to Juliet. "Really?"

"Do you know Hugo?" she asked, thinking that if Paris did, he'd know Hugo was no romantic threat.

"Jana is the one who invited me here tonight," he said,

studying the food in front of him. It was a *foie gras* bonbon with bitter chocolate, pistachios, and cherries.

Funny, Paris said Jana's name, and there Jana stood, next to her mother's chair, and whispering in Saskia's ear.

Juliet didn't know Jana well, other than she was the quiet one of the three younger people in the house. She was Hugo and Mali's cousin, and as far as Juliet could remember, she was Cyril's niece.

Jana dressed simpler than most of the crowd. No flashy crystals and diamonds for her. She wore a flattering white top with sheer sleeves and a tailored pink skirt. A pearl barrette kept her naturally blonde hair to the left side of her oval face.

But, the man, this Noah York person, wow. He was the most handsome man Juliet had ever encountered. Was he thirty-five, thirty-six? His dark hair was too short to slick with pomade. That face, though, perfectly proportioned, slender nose, expressive dark brows–cleft chin. And if that wasn't enough, he was tall and square-shouldered–and tanned. How had he managed that? Noah bent forward to say something in Jana's ear.

Saskia turned to Cyril and said something.

Cyril glanced at Jana. So did Juliet. Something was happening.

"Go hence, to have more talk of these sad things."

Chapter 2

Saskia placed her hands on the table and pushed to her feet.

Cyril jiggled his head, making the rug on his head shimmy. Then he got to his feet fast.

Saskia held up a glass of champagne and tapped it with a fork.

The clinking noise caught everyone's attention, and the room quieted. The orchestra paused.

Saskia raised her voice and her glass. "Hello again, guests and friends. I have an announcement. My niece, Jana Novak, is marrying Noah York. They're engaged."

A cheer went up around the twenty tables, and guests raised their fluted glasses to the couple. People got to their feet.

Eyes wide, Juliet pushed to her feet too and set her napkin on the table. What was happening? Hugo said Noah was breaking up with Jana.

Didn't that just prove that Hugo was nothing but gossip, and all that talk about diddley … diddle … whatever he'd said, was nothing but blather. Juliet searched for him in the crowd.

Shame on you, Hugo!

She didn't see the gossiper, but someone else caught Juliet's attention: Mali. The girl lowered her camera and stared daggers at Noah York.

Noah stood beside Jana with his arm around her waist, drinking in the applause. Cyril leaned around his wife, and Noah shook his hand.

Juliet stood closer to Paris. She nodded toward the other side of the room. "Mali looks put out."

Paris' eyes followed the direction that she'd nodded. He said, "Yeah, because Noah York is now part of the family."

"You know him, too?"

"I know him in a roundabout way," Paris confessed, taking his seat.

Juliet sat too, replacing her napkin in her lap. "Oh, here's some gossip. Some woman claims to have had Noah's baby."

"Which woman?" he asked, moving aside as a waiter placed a salad in front of him. "Noah has a lot of women chasing him."

"That's funny, Hugo said the same thing."

Now, what was the woman's name? It started with a B.

Juliet lifted her fork. After she'd finished a bite of mango, she pointed the other half at Paris. "Hugo said Noah took a paternity test, and it turns out the baby was not his."

Paris nodded and finished the food in his mouth. "Someone should have a talk with Jana about her choice in men."

* * *

Six weeks later, Juliet returned home from Matera, Italy. She was so ready to sleep in her bed, on the Saatva mattress, and to tangle in the white linen bedding. She'd missed her balcony and the view in the evening when the sun lingered in the west over Lake Erie and turned the sky red and orange.

And she missed Paris Nobleman.

Dressed in a pink and gray cable knit sweater and ragged-leg jeans, Juliet sat in one of the chairs on the balcony with her ankle boots crossed in front of her. The vines in the surrounding fields were in *Bloom*. Bloom only happened for two weeks in the springtime, and the developing grape clusters had flowered. The scent was apple-like, subtle, and fleeting.

She'd come out on the balcony to drink chardonnay and return Paris' phone call. When he picked up, there was a hollow sound in the background and an engine noise too. She asked, "Are you driving?"

"I'm coming back from the Novaks', yeah?"

"Again?"

"My sister is visiting and wanted to see Jana."

"Portia's here?" Juliet brought her boots beneath the

chair and leaned forward. "Is she coming back with you?"

"No, she stayed with the Novaks." Paris must've pressed the gas again because the hum of the engine grew louder. "She's trying to talk Jana out of marrying Noah York."

Juliet ran a finger along the top of her wine glass on the table. It seemed as though everyone knew Noah and clearly hated him – except for Jana. "How do you know the guy?"

"Through mutual friends of my family."

"Really? Hugo said something about Xenia bringing him back from a volcano … or something."

"He calls himself a professional adventurer and hooks up with any lady with money who'll financially back his indulgences."

Juliet let her back hit the chair again. "What sort of indulgences?"

"Mountain climbing, biking across Europe. He once walked across the Chihuahuan Desert."

"That's absurd, walking across a desert…" Juliet lifted her ankle and balanced it on her knee. "I would've liked to have met your sister."

"You will meet her another day. I want to see you alone first."

Juliet smiled without realizing it. "Come for dinner. We're eating Chicken Parmigiana. *Nonna* wants to prove she's just as good a cook as the old men in Matera."

"Is she as good?"

"She's better, but she felt challenged after we ate at the *Vitantonio Lombardo Ristorante. Cosi bueno!*"

He was silent for a moment. "You've come back more Italian than when you left."

"I've always been one hundred percent Italian."

"I want to see you alone," he said, his voice dropping an octave. "Meet me for coffee on Monday?"

For some stupid reason, her heart picked up speed. At first, it had been strolling along, now it was power walking. "Sure," she told him.

"Hey, I've got another call. I'm off, love, yeah?"

Juliet turned off the phone and laid her head against the back of the chair. She'd really wanted Paris to come for dinner. But apparently, he was busy. Paris seemed fully-scheduled of late but doing what, exactly? It was almost as though he had another life.

And what responsibilities was he always mentioning? Also, why couldn't Juliet meet his sister? Portia had visited twice since Paris moved to Verona's Vineyard, and for this reason or that, Juliet had never met her.

Those seemed like questions worth asking.

Standing, she moved toward the railing. A fresh wind blew her curls off her face. She'd speak to Paris on Monday and begin her investigation into his life.

* * *

On Sunday, Juliet returned to church with her grandmother Tribly.

St. Mary's was the centerpiece of Verona's Vineyard, like a water feature in a garden where all the birds flocked. Two bell towers, on the south and north, rang at different times during the day. The south bell rang out at noon to call all the faithful to recite the Lord's Prayer. The north bells rang that morning for the preparation for Holy Communion.

The church was the first building constructed in

Verona's Vineyard, outside the actual vineyards. Inside the church were tapestries so old that their color had faded. Mariotto Romeo had bought them from an ancient church in Rome, and they'd hung in St. Mary's for more than twenty years. Juliet's favorite was the Rafael, the Miracle of the Draught of Fishes. The blue threads were still vibrant though the rest had deteriorated from too much light.

Once the service concluded, Juliet stood at the front pew, waiting for her grandmother.

Tribly collected her Bible and turned to Juliet. She lifted a crooked finger and boomed, "He's going to propose."

It was a finishing statement to a conversation they'd started during Concluding Rites.

Juliet glanced around her to see if everyone had heard Tribly.

Of course they had because the old woman never spoke quietly. Her voice was always, always at the number ten setting on any volume button. Then, in a poetic and ominous tone, she said, "You will say no."

"You've had a vision?"

Her wrinkly eyes wrinkled more. "No, I'm telling you not to marry Paris Nobleman. He's not Italian."

Juliet adjusted the purse strap on her shoulder. She wore a peacock colored, wide swinging skirt with a long sleeve navy top, and a double belt draped on her waist. "If I want to …"

"I'm your *Nonna*, and I said no." Nodding her dyed black hair, she shuffled toward the end of the pew. She'd worn her usual Sunday black dress with a white sweater overtop, the one with the little pearls cascading down the front. A lace prayer shawl covered the back part of her head.

Juliet followed her grandmother. "It doesn't matter.

Paris is not going to propose. He knows I'm not ready to marry anyone."

Tribly stopped all forward movement. She pivoted in her orthopedic shoes. "Why not? *Dios Mio*, you still love that police boy!"

"It's not that," Juliet said, her shoulders wilting.

Tribly narrowed her eyes and leaned in. She was only five foot tall, but she was a mean old biddy sometimes. "You can't marry him either."

"Nicolo is Italian."

"That Montague boy is only half Italian. The English side of him arrested your father last year. What sort of blood would he bring to our family?"

Before Juliet could fathom an answer, a woman with Margaret Thatcher hair stepped toward them, meeting them in the center aisle. "*Buongiorno*." It was Abram Fontana's mother. She used to be taller, maybe five foot three, but today if she said she was five foot, she'd be lying. On her nose sat a pair of silver rimmed glasses with dark lenses. They were transitional eyewear that didn't work correctly. Her name was Anna– Anna Fontana.

Si.

Anna turned her dark eyeglasses on Juliet. "*Ciao.* How are you?"

"I'll tell you how she is," Tribly shouted. "She can't make a commitment."

Anna shook her head and made a 'tsk, tsk' sound.

Juliet's eyes drifted left, and then she winced. "What?"

"She has a man in each hand and doesn't want to let one go."

Anna nodded. "To be so lucky."

"I do *not* have a man in each hand."

"Commitment," Tribly said, raising her crooked finger again. "Make up your mind and stick to it, *sì?*" She threw out her hand. "Commit to it."

"Your *nonna* is right," Anna said, switching her pocketbook onto her other arm.

Tribly stepped closer to Juliet. She smelled like Ponds Cold Cream, with a hint of rosemary and garlic. "Your *nonno* wasn't the only man I loved, *sì?* I didn't marry him for a long time. But I chose Italian. I chose blood." She patted her sagging breast. "He was penniless when I met him, and he had a big nose. I never saw such a big nose."

Anna nodded as if she knew the story already.

"He came to New York from Matera. I didn't like him. Other men had more money and smaller noses. But the other men, they grew up Irish and Nazi. Madonna! One was from Barcelona." She angled even closer, as though she meant to whisper. "I'd die before I marry a man from Barcelona," she shouted. "They're not good lovers. Stay away from the Garcias and the Iglesias."

Juliet glanced around the sanctuary. Most of the congregation was near the exit and shuffling outside. All but Finn Mayer, who waited on the other side of the aisle for Tribly.

Did Nonna just call him a Nazi?

Anna said, "My son Abram, he is Italian."

I'll pass, thanks.

"*Sì*, Abram is good. It's good he never arrested my Santos." Tribly nodded and then tilted her head toward Anna. "He makes money with the insurance business, no?"

Hard pass!

"Abram is only a friend," Juliet told the ladies.

Anna said, "Friends make the best husbands, I know."

"Right. Well," Juliet said, turning toward her grandmother. "I'm going to meet Emma for lunch. I'll see you at home."

Tribly raised her hand and waved. "Stay away from anyone named Ruiz!"

* * *

Juliet didn't bother with her car and walked the small distance from the church to the restaurant. The air had warmed to fifty-five degrees, mostly because the sun hit the main road, and the cobblestones baked like a thousand loaves of bread, between the shops and restaurants. The wind off Lake Erie was crisp as it sifted the dogwood flowers and wisteria blossoms. The town was a tourist spot, built to resemble the ancient village of Taormina, Italy. It had been built on a hill so that businesses off Via Lazzaretto were only accessible through hidden alleyways and oversized wooden doors.

The *Vineria Modi Bistro* was near the two-story gazebo, and outdoor seating and blue-striped umbrellas filled the courtyard. The owner had set out heat lamps to warm the square pattern of tables and chairs.

Juliet started with the Beef Tartare with Provola cream, and black truffles washed down with red wine. She'd moved into the *primi piati*, or the first course, of homemade *Maccheroni* with asparagus and clam sauce.

Emma sat across the round table, digging in just as heartily as Juliet. To them, to all Italians really, the afternoon meal was the most important of the day. Emma said, "I received my invitation to Jana Novak's wedding." She was dressed in an embroidered keyhole top, jeans, and knee-high red suede boots.

"When is it?"

"August something," the girl said, taking another sip of wine. The sunshine streaming through the blue-striped umbrella turned her lavender hair nearly blue. It worked for her because she wore the same shade of lipstick.

"Do you know much about Noah York?"

"Other than he's hot?" Emma asked. She shook her head. "No."

A police cruiser caught Juliet's attention. It passed the alleyway at a slow speed, as if the officer was looking for someone. She turned her attention back to the conversation. "Hugo said that Noah's a womanizer."

"Hugo is so dramatic."

"He is, but Paris said the same thing."

"Did he?" Emma took another bite of pasta and then pointed her fork at Juliet while chewing. Swallowing, she asked, "How is Paris?"

Taking a long breath, she pushed at the food on her plate with her fork. "I think he's fine. I'll see him tomorrow. He said he wants to talk to me about something." She twisted her shoulder and said in a sultry voice, "He wants to be alone with me." Then she grinned and picked up her wine glass.

Emma ran her tongue across her teeth for a moment, thinking about it, and then announced, "He's going to propose."

Juliet thudded the wine glass on the table. "Okay, *Nonna*."

"Oh, so Tribly thinks so too?" She leaned across the table, eyes bright. "Will you say yes?"

"No, I will not."

"But Paris is divine." Emma sat straighter in her chair.

"Is this about Nicolo?"

"No, Tribly, it's not."

"I'm channeling your grandmother. That means I'm right, right?"

Juliet shook her head and watched the main road again—and the police cruiser slowly passed the entrance once more.

Emma practically sang her response, "Oh, this is soooo about Nicolo. You haven't forgiven him, but you love him."

"I have forgiven him."

She lowered her lids. "But you won't date him."

Juliet puffed out her cheeks and let a slow breath. "Not since last October, no."

The girl shook her head, as though crestfallen again. Emma really needed to pick a team. "Why not? I mean, since you've forgiven him and all is back to the way it was."

How to explain?

"I always get the idea that I disappoint Nicolo. He disapproves of everything I say and do. It all started last summer when I proposed to him."

Emma dropped her fork.

It hit the table and clattered onto the stone flooring.

The girl made a dive for it.

Juliet bent to the side and met Emma halfway. "He said no."

Emma sat straight again and chose another fork to eat more pasta. "I think he regrets saying no."

"I doubt it."

"I've seen the way he looks at you." She raised the new fork. "Remember when we ice skated with that little man …?"

"Abram."

"Right. Nicolo was there too. I saw his face when he looked in your direction. He was all puppy eyed and yearning for affection from you."

Juliet pushed her plate away and set her fork aside. "Even if Nicolo still cares about me, he acts angry over whatever I'm up to at the moment."

"Solving murder cases that he's working on?"

"Er, yes. But, I'm a curious person, and I doubt I'll change that habit anytime soon. Nicolo will always get fed up with my curio—"

"Nosiness?"

Juliet winced. "Whatever."

Emma pushed her plate away too and raised her hand for the waiter. "And Paris? Does he get upset with your investigative ways?"

"No, he does not."

The waiter stood at the table. His name, Vitale. He had long wavy brown hair that was brushed off his forehead, and he wore black framed glasses. Pretty Vitale. In a thick accent, he asked, "The *dolce*, what will it be?"

Juliet answered first, "*Il Cannolo alla ricotta*," which was a cannoli with sweet ricotta cheese.

Emma ordered the Tiramisu with mascarpone cream.

Vitale gave them a clipped nod and moved away.

Juliet went on, "My problem with Paris is that he's so secretive."

Emma actually leaned backward with the words—as if the sentence were a wave pushing her into her chair. "But, he's so obviously in love with you. He's not hiding secrets."

"No," Juliet said, holding up the palm of her hand and shaking her head. "He keeps me out of his most private issues. He tells me he has responsibilities, but won't tell me what they are. I've never met his parents or his sister."

Emma nodded. "Right. Has he ever told you why he moved away from Martha's Vineyard and away from the family fortune?"

"You see?" Juliet's back hit her chair too. "That, right there. He won't open up about his split with his parents."

"Have you asked him straight out?"

The question took away some of Juliet's steam. "Not exactly, but I plan to tomorrow when I see him. I promise you that."

* * *

She returned to the church parking lot, watching clouds approaching from the west. They were tall, puffy white, but underneath, dark gray and heavy with rain. Juliet climbed into the Fiat and turned her phone back on.

Starting the engine, she pulled the car onto Piazza Duomo. Already, shop lights blinked and streetlamps clicked on, too.

The ringtone on her cell played, and Juliet glanced at the passenger seat and at the phone display: Loved Enemy.

It meant Nicolo Montague was on the other end of the line.

Juliet had never changed the secret name for him. She'd never been able to wipe Nicolo out forever. Pushing the talk button, she asked, "Have you caught your man?"

He said nothing for a moment, and then, "What?" His tenor voice held a suspicious note.

The traffic light up ahead turned yellow, and Juliet pressed the brake pedal. At the stop, she said, "I was eating lunch and saw you prowling Verona's Vineyard in your cruiser."

"I was looking for you."

She frowned through the windshield at the aspen trees on the hillside. "Were you?"

"I called you." His tone held a hint of impatience as if he thought she'd been avoiding his call.

"I just turned the phone …"

"I need to see you. Is Paris with you?"

"No." The light turned green, and she pressed the accelerator.

"Meet me at Wake-Up Café?"

Juliet backed off the gas pedal. "Now?"

"Yes."

When she got off the phone, she made a left turn and drove toward Via Lazzaretto again. The storm was closer now and a gust rocked the little Fiat. Parking next to the police cruiser, Juliet got out of the car right in front of the café. Nicolo's backside was visible through the plate glass window. He waited in line, three deep, wearing his uniform of khaki cargo pants and a long sleeved black polo shirt. At six foot two, he tended to stand out, but he was also blonde and square-shouldered, and trim through the hips. So, he had a tendency to stand out anyway.

The Wake-Up was a small café with seating areas and benches, and a large front window with views of St. Mary's two bell towers. Its black and chrome color scheme had a youthful feel to it, rather than the old-world atmosphere in the rest of the town. Juliet waited at one of the bistro tables and slung her purse over the chair back before climbing into the tall seat.

Nicolo held two coffee cups when he turned around. His pale blue eyes locked onto hers, and he lifted his brows in recognition. He set an Affogato in front of Juliet.

"Thank you," she said. "You remembered."

He didn't sit, but stood at the table, close to her. "Of course I remember." There was a softness in his features that Juliet hadn't seen in a while.

"How are you, Nicolo?"

"Good," he said with a nod.

She held his eyes; she could stare into the blue forever. But that wouldn't do, would it? There was always such tension between them now. Yes, she'd forgiven Nicolo for *moving on* and dating Roseline within a couple of days of saying goodbye. He'd never been in love with Juliet. And, Juliet had never truly loved him. All they'd had was a powerful attraction to each other. Even now, she felt it, felt the tug of her heart wanting to love him.

Does he feel it too?

"I'm looking for Paris Nobleman."

Evidently not.

"You said you were looking for me."

With half closed eyes, he tilted his chin. "Wherever you are, Paris is not far behind."

"That's true sometimes. But I've been in Italy for the past six weeks."

With his elbow resting on the table, Nicolo put his chin in his hand and absently rubbed his bottom lip with his thumb. "Have you seen him since you've come home?"

"I spoke to him." She'd placed her phone on the table and now held it up to show him.

"May I see that?" he asked, nodding. He'd tied his long blonde locks into a knot at the nape of his neck.

She let him take the phone from her hand. "What's going on?"

Nicolo tapped the display and then flicked his finger to find an app he was interested in. "A woman was murdered at the Porta di Mezzo Hotel in Mayville."

"What's that got to do with Paris?" she asked, watching him sort through the apps.

"He was at the scene." Nicolo stopped at the Messenger app and tapped the screen.

"So?"

"He was in her room, leaning over her lifeless body when a maid opened the door. When the maid screamed, Paris ran."

"O me, what fray was here? Yet tell me not, for I have heard it all."

Chapter 3

Every muscle in Juliet's body froze.

Nicolo continued to flick the screen with his index finger.

Her jaw hurt from clenching her teeth hard. "No, Nicolo, no. You're not allowed to accuse someone I love of murder. Not again."

His eyes lifted. "You love Paris?"

Huh?

She shook her head and shrugged at the same time. "As a friend."

"Stuck in the friend zone, is he? I can't say I'm sorry."

"Just – just don't accuse Paris of murder."

Nicolo was a man of limited movement. His expression didn't alter. "Why not?"

Leaning forward in the seat until her ribs pressed the table, she reminded him, "Because you keep getting it wrong. My father, Anthony…"

"You mean like the way *you* keep getting it wrong?" His eyes were chips of ice. "It's all going down at the library right now. That kind of wrong?"

That doused her campfire a little. "Em, yes, that kind."

He pressed forward, too, and because of his height, he leaned farther across the table than Juliet. He was nearly nose-to-nose with her. "For the record, I didn't arrest your father. Detective Escalus arrested him. And as for Anthony, nobody in their right mind thinks Anthony Yeager is innocent of anything. Someday I'll prove it."

Juliet pressed her back into the metal chair. "None of this has anything to do with Paris."

"I just want to speak to him, Juliet." His attention returned to her phone again. "You and Paris texted a lot while you were in Italy. What was he doing while you were away?"

She lifted a shoulder. "His usual thing. He has responsibilities."

"Like what?"

Good. Right. Fabulous question.

"Just things." She moved the espresso cup closer to her. "His sister Portia was here, and they visited Erie together."

He blinked twice, very fast. "Did they?"

"We have mutual friends there, the Novaks."

"The Novaks? Jana?"

"Yes …" she answered with caution. "You know Jana?"

"I've only seen her once." Setting her phone on the table, he pushed it toward her. "Will you tell me if Paris reaches out to you?"

"Do you want me to call him right now?"

"Um, sure."

Juliet twisted in her seat and pressed Paris' icon on the screen. With her free hand, she straightened the string of the tie around her waist. "Hi Paris, call me when you get a minute." Clicking off, she glanced at Nicolo again.

His forearms were on the table and he'd tilted his head, waiting.

Juliet bit her bottom lip and texted Paris: *Hey, call me.*

Nicolo pushed on the table and stood straighter. "Will you tell me if he calls you back?"

"Of course," she said, swinging her legs to the right and hopping from the seat. She followed Nicolo out of the café and onto the sidewalk. A chilly wind blew the fabric awnings on the storefronts. Juliet asked, "Who was the woman who died in Mayville?"

He stopped beside the cruiser with his hand on the door handle. "Her name hasn't been released yet."

"Anybody I know?"

"I doubt it. She was on vacation, or so I understand." He opened the car door and then leaned his forearm on the top of the doorframe. "She was from New England somewhere."

Juliet wrinkled her nose. "Vacationing in Mayville?"

"Yes."

Juliet shifted her weight and adjusted her purse strap. "It's just not the first place I'd choose to vacation." She swung her hand out, the one holding the coffee cup. "Verona's Vineyard, sure, but Mayville?"

Nicolo's mouth formed a straight line, and he pushed his arm off the doorframe. "Oh, here we go."

"What? It's strange."

He pointed one finger at her. "No, it isn't."

"Oh come on. Mayville isn't the Caribbean."

"She was visiting her family."

"And she stayed in a hotel?" She shook her head. "Weirder and weirder."

His hands on his waist now, he barked, "Stay out of this Juliet, or I'll arrest you."

Her mouth fell open. "For what?"

He reached into the car and took a pair of leather gloves from the dashboard. "You'll go undercover, or you'll break into a house," he explained, fitting one glove on his hand. "You'll point your finger in the wrong direction again."

"I figure things out eventually."

He shook his head and concentrated on the second glove. "You can't be lucky all the time."

"Right," she said, nodding. "Well, thank you for the Affogato."

* * *

Sitting in the Fiat, Juliet placed the coffee tumbler in one of the cup holders between the seats. She clutched the steering wheel and gazed out the windshield. What had Paris been doing at the Porta di Messa with a dead person?

He has responsibilities…

Well, that was a remarkable responsibility. Had he found himself in a Hamlet situation and avenged someone?

Juliet lifted her index fingers off the wheel and tap-tap-tapped like a snare drummer on the march. It was possible.

She herself had sworn to avenge people in the past. Mostly it'd been her cousin Ty who'd asked her to pay back any party responsible for his murder–because there had been plenty of people who wanted to kill him in the past. At times Juliet had been tempted to do it herself.

But Paris wasn't as tragic as Ty.

After buckling her seatbelt, Juliet stretched and rubbed the top of her stomach. It'd turned sour. Perhaps it was from drinking espresso so soon after eating dessert. *Or*, she was sick with the thought of the police arresting someone she loved *again*.

Why it hadn't even been a year since they'd arrested her father, and what, six months since Anthony had been thrown in jail for murder.

Juliet turned the ignition and revved the engine. Someone needed to nip this situation in a hurry.

Backing the car, she made a U-turn in front of St. Mary's, and then followed the main road out of Verona's Vineyard. She drove northward and then east toward Mayville.

Paris had bought a house last January. Not Dr. Dexter's house. All the plans for that arrangement fell through in late November of last year. No, Paris had settled on another house, not far from Dexter's. It was in the same subdivision.

Juliet drove over the bridge and took a left at the first street.

The homes were built along a hillside, and stood catawampus to each other on the cobblestone streets. It reminded Juliet of Venice because a river ran right through the neighborhood. Arched bridges connected the main roads.

The sky was even darker now and had followed Juliet all the way from Verona's Vineyard. The clouds swirled low and threatened snow, blotting out the late afternoon sun. Lights popped on inside the three-story homes. Lamplights flickered along the streets.

Juliet pulled into the driveway of the last house on the cul-de-sac and let the car idle for a few moments.

Where were the police? Shouldn't they be pounding on Paris' door?

Juliet stepped out of the Fiat and took the uphill walk to the front door. At one time, Paris promised her a key to the house, but had yet to hand one over. Not that she'd ever enter his home on a whim … unless there was a medical emergency or he'd killed someone and was on the lam.

She hit the doorbell five times. Yes, five. Make that six. If Paris was home, Juliet wanted him to know how agitated she was at the situation.

Leaning her ear to the door, she listened.

All was quiet.

Juliet followed the pathway again and skirted the side of the house, to the garage door. She peeked through the window.

There was Paris' blue Jaguar.

He has to be inside the house.

Juliet returned to the Fiat and rummaged through her bag for her wallet. Oh, she knew how to break into a house when the occasion called for it.

A door shut somewhere nearby. It was a small noise–as though someone was careful about it.

Juliet dropped the purse and walked to the edge of the driveway.

A lean-built, dark-haired someone ran around the side

of the house next door, took a running leap at the white vinyl fence, scrambled over the top of it, and then dropped out of sight in the neighbor's backyard.

Paris?

A ball of anger ping-ponged around in Juliet's belly. Paris had run from her!

Running for the fence, Juliet sprang forward, hands outreached…

Her fingers missed the top by several inches, and her body slammed hard into the fence. In a squeaky voice, she let out, "I'm fine."

She dropped off the fence and glanced behind her and then up at the windows next door. Had anyone seen her?

Juliet's cheeks heated. How sure she'd been in her ability to hop the fence. How mistaken she ended up being.

How woeful.

The wind swirled faster, and Juliet wrapped her sweater closer around her body. Her arm touched her ribcage and a dull pain shot through her.

"Oww," she complained. She'd definitely need to play on easy mode for a bit. Bending at the waist, Juliet stuck her face against the gate. She adjusted her angle so that she might see between the lock and the post. "Paris Nobleman, come back here right now."

Had he hopped the fence on the other side of the yard?

"Paris, I've broken my ribs. Come and help me."

Nothing.

Juliet hobbled back to the car, flung her purse aside, and slammed the door. She started the engine and backed out of the drive. Driving slowly, she rounded the cul-de-sac and made it to the end of the road.

A police car crossed the bridge. Another vehicle, an

unmarked vehicle, had pulled into the grass on the left side of the road.

The block is hot!

Pressing the gas pedal, Juliet drove away at a law abiding speed.

* * *

The next morning at ten, Juliet stepped inside the Wake-Up Café. The place smelled of vanilla and coffee beans. At least twenty people sat at tables or stood in line. Clinking spoons punctuated the low noise of the grinder machines.

Not ordering her usual, Juliet watched out the front window willing a blue Jaguar to pull into a parking space. She had no idea if Paris meant to keep their coffee date. He'd wanted to speak to her about something, wanted to tell her while they were alone. Juliet was sure Paris had no intention of proposing to her as Tribly and Emma suggested.

Had he meant to tell her about a woman?

Paris met someone…

Her heart gave a lurch.

You don't know that.

She'd tried over and over to call Paris last night. Had he dumped his phone? Juliet would've got rid of hers if she'd murdered someone. That'd be a number one reaction.

Where would I run?

Juliet stood still and took a deep breath. First, she didn't believe Paris killed anyone. He might be on the run, but only to prove himself innocent. And second, *where* would he run to prove himself innocent?

To his sister? Was Portia still at the Novaks – or would she leave the Blonde Palace to help Paris?

I'd return to the scene of the crime to find new evidence.

Right.

Would he be at the scene, lurking about, and hunting for clues?

Juliet snatched her hobo bag from the bench and walked out of the café.

* * *

The Porta Di Messa was a five-story salmon colored building overlooking Lake Chautauqua. A pink and white striped awning covered the walkway to the double doors. Beneath the filigreed name of the hotel was: Flavio Esposito, proprietor.

Through the doors, terracotta tiles led to a red and black themed reception area. Glass and chrome winked beneath the fancy, swirled pendant lights.

Avoiding that particular area, she made for the carpeted staircase on the right side of the room. Wow, so much red carpeting. A wrought iron banister traveled up one side of the steps, and on the other side was a wall of Italian marble. This was no pocket-friendly place that Flavio Esposito owned.

She hadn't dressed for such opulence. She'd worn a black turtleneck and pants, and black boots. Her brown leather trench coat might work if she needed to fit in here for some reason. Juliet hadn't gone for a sophisticated look that morning, more of a *cute* style for Paris' sake.

On the second floor landing, Juliet paused and gazed down the long hallway. She wasn't exactly sure where she'd find Paris. Perhaps he'd stay close to the room where the woman had been murdered.

How to find the room… had the police taped everything off?

Juliet traveled halfway down the hallway and then turned toward the stairs again. On the third floor was a housekeeping cart stacked with fluffy white towels–but no yellow tape pointing out a murder scene.

On the fourth floor, a man approached the stairs just as Juliet was near the top. He wore a staff uniform, green vest, white shirt, and maroon pants.

"Can I help you?"

She hadn't thought too far ahead, and for a flash second, Juliet was flustered. Then she straightened her shoulders and, in her best Saskia Novak voice, said, "You are one of my employees, and you don't know how to ask a question?"

The man jerked to a halt with his thick black brows raised. He was hawk-nosed, eagle-eyed, and possibly bad-tempered. That was merely a guess based on the snarl on his upper lip. "Excuse me?" His name badge read Stefano.

"It's *may* I help you, not *can* I help you." She narrowed her eyes. "Unless you doubt your ability to help me."

Stefano turned his face partially aside, as though not sure what was happening. "*May* I help you?"

"Yes, Stefano," she told him, winging it. "I want to know what took place on the fifth floor."

Oh yes, she was guessing.

He lifted his pointy chin, "I'm not allowed to discuss it with the guests."

"I'm glad to hear that, but I'm not one of your guests, am I? My name is Juliet Esposito." She dragged out the word Esposito, really giving the *PO* a hard landing.

Stefano's dark eyes shifted left and then right, as though he were suddenly nervous.

Oh my God, that worked!

She went on, "My father, Flavio, asked me to find out what is going on here." She quirked her mouth to one side and half hooded her eyes. "What is going on here, Stefano?"

"You mean the murder?"

She gave him a sharp nod.

"Well," he glanced left and right again. "How do you mean? A lady was killed. I don't know what else to say."

She took a step toward him in confidence and lowered her voice. "Here's the problem, as my father, Flavio, sees it. This hotel will lose a lot of money if this situation repeats itself. Was the murder the work of a serial killer?"

He leaned away, hand across his chest. "No!"

"So, you know who killed the woman then?"

"Of course not." He took a step toward the staircase and motioned with his hand. "Let me get the manager for you."

"Is this a joke to you, Stefano?" she asked, keeping her voice rich with Saskia's attitude. "I don't need your manager. I want to speak to whomever witnessed the murder."

His lip lifted above his incisors. "Lucinda only saw the man run away. She didn't see the murder."

Juliet glanced down the long red-carpeted hallway. "Where is Lucinda now?"

"She's cleaning rooms," Stefano said, pointing to the floor above them. "Upstairs."

She stood straighter. "Escort me to Lucinda."

Stefano didn't move.

Oh, he was pushing Saskia!

Juliet took a steady breath. "Now, please."

His chest deflated, and he turned toward the stairs.

A housekeeper's cart stood outside of room 502. Juliet glanced farther down the hallway and saw yellow tape across one of the doors. Fingerprint dust stuck to the side of the wall by the seal.

Stefano pulled a badge key from his pocket and flashed it at the card reader. Opening it, he called "Lucinda."

"Ai!" a woman screamed from inside the room, as though he'd surprised her.

"Come into the hallway," he said with a weary tone to his voice. "Someone wants to ask you some questions." He nodded and seemed about to move toward the stairs again.

Juliet held out her hand. "Stay with us, Stefano."

He closed his eyes, summoning his patience, it seemed, as though he wasn't on board yet with Juliet being the boss' daughter. But he wasn't sure, was he? He pushed his shoulder against the frame of the door and waited.

A woman bustled out of the room. She was sixty something and dressed in a maroon dress with a white collar. Lucinda was about the same height as Tribly.

The fact caused Juliet to relax. She knew how to speak to a *nonna*. With more respect in her tone, she said, "Tell me what happened the day you saw the murder, *si*?

Lucinda's dark eyes widened. "*Si*, murder."

"She didn't see the murder," Stefano reminded her.

Juliet ignored him. "Tell me what happened, Lucinda."

The woman nodded. "I came to the room, *si*? The door, she was cracked." Lucinda pointed to knob. "I announced myself because I heard someone moving in the room."

Juliet studied the door handle and then the hinges. "How was the door cracked when they close automatically?"

"Maybe it hadn't finished closing," Stefano said, distracted by the hem of his vest.

Juliet asked, "What happened next?"

"I saw a man," Lucinda said slowly. "He stood over a dead woman, and I screamed." She nodded and said quickly, "Because I have never seen the dead."

"Never?"

"No, my *matri* and *papa* are still alive."

Juliet asked Stefano, "Does the dead woman have a name?"

"Bexley Pemberton-Kerr."

I've heard that name. Where have I…?

Juliet gasped. "Bexley?"

"You can't lose a game if you don't play the game."

Chapter 4

P emberton-Kerr," Stefano repeated in a bored tone.
Hugo spoke of Bexley. She'd stalked Noah York and Jana. Juliet eyed Lucinda again. "What happened when you screamed?"

She raised her beefy shoulders. "The man ran away."

"He didn't say anything to you?"

"No," Lucinda said, her voice going up with the word the longer she held it.

"Are you sure?" Juliet asked, leaning forward. "He didn't say, 'calm down and let's call the police … yeah?'"

That struck the old woman's memory. Her eyes

brightened. "Oh, he did say something, *sì*." Her gaze went to Stefano. "I will speak to the police again?"

Juliet straightened her shoulders. "You need to tell me first, do you understand?" She gazed at Stefano. "If there is a serial killer here, we'll shut this hotel down. You will lose your jobs."

Stefano's Adam's apple bobbed in the barrel of his throat, and he nodded to the maid.

Lucinda stepped closer. "The man said, 'I didn't kill her. Stop screaming.' Then he said something about his car."

Juliet frowned. "His Jaguar?"

"No, no, his Porsche."

Her mouth dropped open. "Portia?"

"*Sì*," Lucinda said, nodding her tightly wound curls. "Porsche."

Staring at the ceiling for a moment, Juliet said, "Paris did not kill Bexley Pemberton-Kerr."

Stefano pushed off from the wall, his face a mask of suspicion. "How could you possibly know that? And who's Paris?"

"I know because the door was cracked," she told him, pointing at the hinges. "It hadn't shut. That means he'd just walked into the room."

"Then why did he run?"

Juliet lifted a shoulder. "Why didn't he kill Lucinda while he was at it?"

The maid touched her neck with her fingers.

Juliet drove the point home, "Why didn't he shut you up so that there'd be no witnesses?"

"Oh, *sì*," Lucinda said. "Madonna!"

Juliet pursed her lips for a moment, and then asked,

"How did you know the woman was dead? You said you'd never seen a dead person before."

Lucinda still had her fingers on her throat. "Her eyes were opened, and her lips were blue." She glanced down the hallway, toward the murder scene. "Her skin was white. There was something around her neck. A balloon…"

Juliet held up her palm. "Did you say balloon?"

"*Sí,*" Lucinda said. "The tie, you know the tie? It was around her neck."

"Strangled? But, how did you know it was a balloon ribbon?"

"Because the balloon…" Lucinda nodded and made a circle motion with her hand. "She was still attached to the strings. Big fat lips."

Juliet never had this much trouble communicating with Tribly. "What?"

Stefano explained, "It was one of those mylar type balloons, shaped like kissing lips."

Juliet opened her mouth in a silent *Oh.*

"The Kiss of Death," Stefano added with a touch of drama.

"Right," Juliet said. "Did the surveillance cameras show someone toting balloons into the hotel?"

"I don't know," Stefano admitted with a shrug. "The police have the information."

"Do you have cameras here in the hallway?" Juliet asked, gazing toward the crown moldings.

Stefano straightened his vest, importantly. "You don't know that, *Senorita* Esposito?"

She lifted her chin. "Well, I haven't studied the schematics recently."

Stefano narrowed his eyes again—as though he was

about to blow the case wide open. "You come with me to speak to the manager."

"I don't need to," Juliet told him, tightening the sash of her coat and ready to make a quick getaway.

"Stay right here," he told her and turned toward the stairs.

Juliet's chest tightened. Stefano was just the type to call the police while he searched for the manager. She smiled at Lucinda. Keeping her voice calm, she asked, "Where is the fire escape?"

"Why do you want to escape?"

"Maybe that's how the man got out of here."

The maid widened her eyes and glanced down the hallway. She shook her head. "I will get into trouble. Something is wrong with you." She backed toward the door and stuck one foot inside the room.

Juliet didn't wait around to persuade her. She'd find the exit on her own. It was easy enough because there was a sign at the end of the hallway.

Once inside the echoing stairwell, she descended the steps fast and pulled her keys out of her purse at the same time.

And then she dropped them.

The metal ring and keys clattered between the open-ended steps and fell to the second floor.

Juliet took the stairs faster.

She scooped the keys into her hand–and saw something in the corner of the stairwell. Picking it up off the floor, Juliet turned it over in her hand.

It was a ticket. On the front was a photo of a pair of white cockatoos clutching a man's outstretched arm. Written across the top, were the words, Erie Zoo Bird Show.

Stuffing it into her purse, Juliet went out the side door and into the sunshine again.

* * *

Back home, and in the media room on the second floor of the house, Juliet sat at one of the computers and pulled up the name Bexley Pemberton-Kerr. She found Bexley's name, but no photos. She learned the Pemberton-Kerrs were a prominent family in the Boston area. They were *old money* in the steel business.

Juliet sat back in the office chair and swiveled back and forth.

How did Paris know Bexley? Was she the girl he'd met recently? Were they romantically involved? Or… maybe they ran in the same circles back home. Boston and Martha's Vineyard were geographically near one another. It wouldn't be a stretch of the imagination to think they had known each other for some time.

"Hey," a man's voice said behind her.

Juliet spun the chair around.

Her cousin Ty Gatti stood in the glass door entryway.

"Hi. How are you?" She asked because he seemed a bit crestfallen with his droopy brows and slumped shoulders. He looked like that a lot of the time anyway.

"Good," he said, coming all the way into the room and taking a seat on the padded footstool of a paisley armchair. With his long legs bent, he looked like a two-legged spider with black hair.

"How's Delia?"

"Sweet, beautiful," he said, and let out a long breath. "Exciting."

Ty had been crazy about the woman since he'd met her

last November. He'd dug in his heels when Juliet suggested he meet Delia. Ty hadn't wanted anyone to manage Ganozza's bakery after his mother died. But then he took one look at Delia and desired to give her the entire shop, as long as he could work alongside her.

"Why are you laughing?" Ty asked. He had a masculine voice, though it was thick sounding, and he spoke slower than most people. "I'm in love, Juliet."

"Is Delia?"

Elbow on his knee, he put his chin in his hand. "She says I'm too young for her."

"You are."

"What does age have to do with it anyway? You're older, and your love life is pretty derelict."

She furrowed her brows, "I wouldn't call it … derelict."

Gazing at the far wall, he mused, "I suppose you have Paris in your pocket, if you ever looked his way." Then his dark eyes snapped back to Juliet, "Which reminds me, did you lose your phone?"

Still scowling, she blinked a couple of times in confusion. "No."

"Then why did Paris text me to tell you something?"

Her heart jumped to life. So did she, out of the chair that is, and the seat spun around a couple of times. "Paris? What did he say?"

In the manner of a snail, Ty reached for the phone in his pocket. "I'm about to tell you. You're so impatient, Juliet." Still squatting on the footrest, he flipped through the messages on his phone. "He said, "'Ty, it's Paris. Tell Juliet that Jana Novak was murdered.'"

Her mouth fell open. "Jana? Oh, my…" Turning toward the desk again, Juliet pushed the chair aside and pounded away at the keyboard. Then she stared at the screen. "I don't see anything about Jana dying."

"Do you want to hear the rest of the text?"

Juliet spun around and snatched Ty's phone from him. She read the message: "Ask her to meet me at the library and wear her hat."

Off the cushion, Ty snatched his phone back. "Which library? What hat?"

Juliet stared at the bookcase for a moment. "I think he means the West Portland library. I wore a hat there last time we went inside the place."

"Why all the cloak and dagger about it?" Ty put the phone back into his top pocket. "Why can't people just say what they mean? Delia doesn't think I'm too young for her. She's just not attracted to me."

Juliet frowned, not keeping up. "What?"

"I'm going to dance again." With his hand on his stomach, he gyrated his hips. "Show her my moves."

"Right," she told him, heading for the door. "When did you get that text from Paris?"

He still moved his hips and spun in a circle. "Just as I came into the house."

"Good, that's good. What number did Paris call from? Was it his cell phone?"

"I didn't recognize the number."

* * *

Pulling on her leather trench coat, Juliet climbed into the Fiat and then raced northward with her phone to her ear. When her mother didn't pick up, she tossed the phone toward her purse. Had her mother found out already about

Jana? That she'd been murdered?

There would have been signs if Italia knew about the murder. She would've wailed and pulled her hair. And Tribly? She'd ride shotgun on the drama train, circling her cast-iron skillet over her head to ward off the evil eye.

No, no one in the Da Vinci household knew about Jana's death except Ty, and he didn't count because he'd never met the Novaks.

So, how had Paris known about it, especially since he was on the run?

Okay, just to throw it out there: if Paris did kill Bexley, then he might've killed Jana, too. That would explain how he knew about it.

Paris did not kill Bexley or Jana.

Then why had he run from her? Why hop a fence and not answer when she yelled that she'd broken a rib – which, still hurt when she touched it, by the way.

Juliet felt her left side. See? Still hurts.

Changing lanes, she drove toward the Osborne Street exit just ahead of a silver car.

Bexley had been murdered, strangled. And now Jana had been murdered. They had to be related. The girls knew each other, or they at least knew *of* each other.

How did Jana die? There were plenty of ways to go.

With both hands back on the wheel, Juliet ran through a couple of scenarios: Bexley followed Jana because Bexley was stalkerazzi. Then, in a fit of jealousy, Bexley killed Jana, ran from the scene, and killed herself.

With a balloon tie?

Okay, no.

Someone saw Bexley murder Jana, and that someone, motivated by revenge, killed Bexley with a balloon tie.

Why isn't any of this making sense?

It was the balloon idea that kept stumping her. How did someone kill Bexley with a flimsy ribbon?

I think I could fight off a balloon ribbon.

Maybe, the killer strangled Bexley with bare hands and then added the ribbon as a special touch. The balloon was a calling card, in other words.

Had Jana been strangled too? If she was killed the same way, that would connect the two deaths.

Juliet pulled into the left turn lane just ahead of a silver car with a tennis ball on the antenna; a pink tennis ball with ribbons streaming off the bottom of it.

Where have I seen that car?

She thought back. She'd seen it … oh, it had been parked at the Porta di Messa hotel yesterday.

A gasp caught in her throat, and her stomach muscles twisted.

Juliet had seen the car somewhere else, too.

Okay, so either the driver was a teenage girl or was a murderer who had a penchant for ribbons.

A stop sign appeared up ahead. Juliet pressed the brake, and then waited a long moment for the sedan to catch up to her.

The car slowed and stopped behind the Fiat, remaining four or five car lengths behind.

She turned left onto Main.

The speed limit was thirty, but Juliet had already pushed the speedometer to forty-five miles per hour.

Don't try this at home, children.

Main Street was mostly a residential area with one lane that wound its way toward the center of town. There'd be no outrunning the car in this situation. Juliet had tried to do that once before and wound up in a ravine.

Reaching for her purse, she pulled out her phone and the cord that fit into the Fiat's USB. Hitting the Amazon app, Juliet said, "Alexa, how do I lose a tail while driving?"

"You lose a tail by driving like you're drunk," the automated voice answered. "Speed up, slow down, signal one way, and turn another. Drive drunk until you lose the car tailing you."

Juliet straightened in her seat and watched the rearview. "Good. Right." Taking her foot off the accelerator, she let the Fiat drift for a moment.

Up ahead was the courthouse and the jail. She flipped on the left turn signal and crept toward the intersection.

The silver car remained five car lengths back.

At the last second, Juliet swerved right, punched the gas pedal, and flew northward on Academy Road.

The silver sedan swerved right, but then corrected itself at the last minute.

Juliet pressed the brake and slowed again, crossed the yellow line, and then got back into her lane.

The pink tennis ball appeared in the rearview, but, the car remained several car lengths behind the Fiat.

She turned right and then corrected the vehicle into a left turn.

The silver car kept pace.

Juliet signaled right, but took a left, and punched the accelerator. She watched the rearview mirror.

The sedan missed the turn.

Juliet grinned and pushed the Fiat to sixty.

Tires squealed on the pavement in the distance.

The Fiat hit seventy miles per hour, and then Juliet braked into a turn to the right.

A large truck with a red cab had parked on the shoulder of the road up ahead.

Juliet slowed the car, swerved around it, and then hit the brakes. She waited, hidden by the truck. If she could get behind the other vehicle...

The silver car flew past her driver's side window.

Juliet saw the driver this time.

Too late, Nicolo saw the Fiat and slammed on the brakes. His car came to a stop on the shoulder of the road.

Juliet drove onto the road and then pulled even with the sedan. She hit the passenger window button and watched it slide down.

Nicolo already had his driver's side window open. He nodded and said, "Juliet."

"This love feel I, that feel no love in this."

Chapter 5

She bent further over into the passenger seat. "Nice antenna topper," she told him, nodding at the tennis ball.

His mouth was set in a grim smile. "My mother's."

"You're driving her car now? Did the police department run out of unmarked vehicles?"

He lifted his dark brows. "I'm not working right now."

"Really?" She put the Fiat into Drive, pulled ahead of the sedan, and parked on the shoulder of the road. Juliet got out and then walked back to the silver car. She leaned on the doorframe, arms crossed against the cold air, "Why are you following me, Nicolo?"

His pale blue eyes narrowed. He wasn't in uniform, but that didn't mean he wasn't undercover. He asked, "Why are you driving under the influence?"

"I don't drink and drive." The wind was up, and it blew the curls out of Juliet's face. "You think I'll lead you to Paris."

He placed his forearm on the steering wheel. "You've been searching for him."

"Because I'm worried about him."

"I want to believe you." He shifted slightly so that his head leaned out the window. "If anyone will find Paris, it'll be you."

Juliet covered her heart with one hand. "That is the nicest thing you've said to me lately."

His mouth curled downward. "What?"

"You think I'm a good enough detective to find a man on the run. Thank you, Nicolo. That's quite a confidence booster." She bit her lip to keep from smiling.

He shook his blonde hair, again pulled back in a knot at his neck. "Paris is in love with you. He'll reach out." He pushed his hand out the window. "May I see your phone again?"

"It's in my car, plugged in." She didn't move.

"Will you get it?"

She gave him a coy smile and returned to her vehicle and unplugged the phone. Back at the sedan, Juliet handed it over.

Nicolo narrowed his eyes suspiciously. Had he expected her to hem and haw about it; try to hide her phone from him?

See how smart Paris was not to call Juliet's phone? She

appreciated that fact right then.

Swiping the face of the phone, Nicolo stared at the messages and phone call history. "Where are you headed right now?"

"Delia's house," she lied.

Yes, she lied. Why did it come so quickly to her these days? She'd need a confessional seat with her name etched on it soon. She said, "Do you remember Delia? She's Geoff Leary's daughter."

He gave Juliet a quick glance. There was a hint of a surprise there. "She still speaks to you?"

"Yes. We're friends. She runs Ganozza's Bakery for us."

He nodded and looked at the phone again.

"I want her to make pastries for Jana Novak's memorial service."

Nicolo's head whipped back around. "What do you know about that?"

She held up her palms. "I told you that I know the Novaks. My mother is a close friend of Saskia."

"Uh-huh," Nicolo said, shaking his head and catching her eyes again. "I think you said that so I'd know that you know what's going on."

"I didn't."

Of course, I did.

"You want me to think you already know things so that I'll give you information." Nicolo handed the phone back to her. "I'm not on the case, Juliet. The Erie Police are handling Jana's murder. I'm only following leads here in New York for them."

Juliet stuffed the phone into the pocket of her leather coat. "What about Bexley Pemberton-Kerr? She was killed in Mayville. Shouldn't you be investigating her death?"

He shook his head. "Erie took over that as well."

"Wow, you can never catch a break. You finally make detective, and then there are five murders, and you've only investigated one of them."

"Wait a minute, wait a minute," Nicolo said, narrow-eyed and waving one hand. "How did you know Bexley's last name?"

Her mouth hung open for a moment before finally answering, "You know I was at the Porta di Messa yesterday. I saw your tennis ball."

He made a face. "It's not *my* tennis ball." His back hit the seat, and he let his head fall back on the headrest. "Wait a minute, did you impersonate a police officer?"

"Of course not."

"Then how do you know anything?"

Juliet twisted her mouth before confessing, "Stefano might've believed I was the hotel owner's daughter."

Blue eyes seared into hers. "That's unethical."

"But not illegal. I asked Alexa before I went inside." She patted the sedan's window frame. "I've got to dash, Nicolo. Are you coming?"

Not waiting for his answer, she returned to her car, shut the door, and put the car into reverse. After a three-point turn, she pressed the gas and headed back toward Academy Road. She watched the rearview mirror.

The sedan was making the same turn.

Meeting Paris was obviously out of the question at the moment, so Juliet made a right on Main Street and drove toward her home.

Her cell phone rang a few seconds later.

Nicolo said, "I thought you were going to Delia's house."

Juliet frowned at her phone and then placed it to her ear again. "Here's the thing. I forgot what time it is. Delia sleeps in on Sundays."

"Good thing it's Monday."

"Right. Got to go, bye." She said and hung up before he could ask her another question.

* * *

Juliet pulled the Fiat onto the driveway of her family's home. The long brickwork wound through the vineyards for a half a mile, and on either side, field workers dressed the vines in the cold. Farther out were the espalier frames that supported the lemon trees that had harvested over the wintertime. Plenty of limoncellos were now at the West Portland facility and ready to ship to Juliet's balcony.

The house came into view. It was a Mediterranean style, three stories, and older than Juliet. Her father had the home built for Italia, and for Tribly, too. The house was lavish and worthy of any Italian countryside with a courtyard full of Italian pine.

Juliet parked the car, made her way toward the back door–the kitchen entrance–and hung her keys on the rack, just inside the doorway. Santos had built the space to Tribly's specification, and it was like stepping into a cook's kitchen in Matera. Wooden beams, stone walls, and cherry wood cabinets filled the space. A huge island took up the center of the room, and hanging overhead was all manner of pots and utensils and baking equipment.

And, it smelled like fish.

There was Tribly now, her back to Juliet, hammering something with a mallet near the stove.

All at once, Juliet's mother burst through the swinging doors on the other side of the room. She carried a suitcase in her hand.

She's learned about Jana.

"What's going on?" Juliet asked, still at the door.

"Jana Novak is dead," Italia said, pulling leather gloves from the pocket of the long coat she already wore. Setting the suitcase on the terra cotta floor, she fit a glove onto her hand. Her long hair was up in a messy bun with tendrils on either side of her face.

"I heard," Juliet said, her voice full of sympathy. "I'm so sorry."

Italia stopped fussing with her gloves. "How would you know something like that? I just found out."

"The gift," Tribly shouted from the island. She waved a wooden mallet at them. "I told you she has the gift."

Italia's eyes didn't shift from Juliet's. She kept her voice low. "Don't listen to your *nonna*. There is no gift. Now, how did you know Jana is dead?"

"Nicolo told me."

"Why would he tell you that?" she asked, fitting the other glove in place.

"Or I told him, I can't remember," Juliet said. "When is the funeral?" She moved toward the chairs at the kitchen island and then hopped onto one of them.

"No funeral, but they will have a Celebration of Life the day after tomorrow. We're all going."

"With no Pope, there is no celebration," Tribly said, pulling a cast-iron skillet from a cabinet.

"The Pope wouldn't be at the Novaks anyway," Italia reminded her, moving toward the center of the room, too.

"*Si*. The Pope, he would not be caught dead in such

a place." She shook the skillet at Italia. "It is sinful how much they own."

Juliet swiveled her chair and faced her mother, "Why was Jana living with the Novaks? Where are her parents?"

"She is, *was*, Cyril's niece," Italia explained. "Her parents died in a car crash when she was eight years old. According to Saskia, Jana never really fit in with them."

"Wasn't Jana used to the wealthy lifestyle?"

"Oh, I think she was. Her parents were wealthy and left her money. She'd just received the inheritance recently. Saskia thought the girl would go off on her own, but she didn't."

Tribly flopped a fish onto a cutting board on the counter and pulled a fillet knife from a drawer. "Someone killed her for the money," she said, and then made the sign of the cross with a knife still in her hand.

Juliet sat straighter and crossed herself, too.

But, back to her mother, "Do you know how Jana died? Did Saskia say?"

Italia brought her hand to her throat. "Strangled. Saskia thinks she was robbed for the ring that Noah gave to her. It was eighteen carats. Someone pulled her into an alley behind some dive of a Chinese restaurant where she had met her friend Valerie for dinner. The ring was missing from her finger."

"Eighteen carats?" Juliet asked. "How did Noah York afford that on an adventurer's salary? Jana must've bought the ring herself."

Her mother leaned away and narrowed her eyes. "How do you know anything about Noah York?"

"Paris told me."

Her mother's amber eyes lowered, and she dropped

her voice. "Dear, I want you to stop seeing Paris."

"Why?"

She leaned in, glanced over at Tribly, and then whispered. "Because Saskia thinks so. The police asked her all about Paris' visit. She put two and two together, and I think she's onto something. The police think he killed Jana."

Juliet threw out her hands. "Oh, for goodness sake. Saskia is not a police officer. Paris didn't kill Jana."

"Let's just say for a moment that he did."

She spun the chair to face her mother again. "Think about it, *Matri*. Why would Paris kill Jana for a diamond? His family is as wealthy as the Novaks."

"I'm just telling you what the police believe, Juliet. And Paris' family is wealthy, yes, but Paris is not. He's argued with his mother and father."

Juliet put her elbow on the counter and cupped her chin. "Do you know why? Paris has never told me what happened."

Italia lifted a shoulder. "It had something to do with a woman."

The knot returned to Juliet's stomach.

He's seeing someone.

She bit her lip for a moment and then asked, "Was Paris ever involved with Bexley Pemberton-Kerr?"

Italia lifted her chin and laughed. "Pemberton-Kerr? Heavens no. I'm sure Natalie and Marcus would've thrown Paris at Bexley, not disown him over her."

"Have you heard that Bexley died?"

Her mother twisted around and picked up her suitcase again. "I'm sure you're wrong, dear."

"I'm not wrong. Bexley died at the Porta Di Messa

Hotel. Paris was with her."

Italia waved one hand in the air and retreated. "Well, that's another reason for you to not see Paris anymore. I'll see you at the celebration." And then, she walked out of the door.

Juliet stared at her grandmother.

"Celebration of life, bah," the old woman said, pretending to spit in the air. "The only time you celebrate death is when you did the killing, *sì*?"

Juliet nodded thoughtfully. "*Sì.*"

* * *

With traffic, the drive to the Novaks' home from the Da Vinci vineyards took a little over forty-five minutes. Juliet drove her car instead of tagging along with her father and Tribly.

The mansion sat a mile away from the road. On the day of the memorial service, the twelve-foot iron gates remained wide open. Cars then needed to wind along a blacktop road through a pine forest that led to an arched bridge. Beyond the bridge was a gravel parking area. There were also four garages if the weather turned foul.

The weather wasn't foul at all. In fact, it was glorious with the temperature in the high fifties, and the sunshine made everything from the landscape to the windows of the house shine and wink.

Manned golf carts took the guests to the back lawn and dropped them off at the garden entryway. From there, it was a five-minute expedition around the remainder of the house, across stone paths and through rose gardens, and then the lawn opened up to a view of Lake Erie. Rows of white chairs sat in front of a dais with a pulpit on it.

The Novaks enjoyed their lives on a different level than most people. Yes, Juliet came from money, but not the Mansa Musa type of rich that was going on here. For instance, there was an entire wing of the house dedicated to a spa. And for another, there was a ten-foot by thirty-foot waterfall in the rose patch. Did anyone really need eleven swimming pools?

What they lacked here was the coziness of home, the Italian kitchen, and a *nonna* baking bread and making pasta from scratch.

A lot of people had shown up for the service and most were making their way across the lawn toward the white chairs. Many were the same guests who'd attended the Valentine Ball–only now they were dressed in funeral attire instead of flapper and gangster wear.

Juliet wore black too; a high-waist dress with a gold emblem belt, black coat, and black boots that reached her knees. She'd never been on this side of the house and paused to gaze at the infinity pool just a short distance from where she stood. It was a tiered pool that went along the entire east and south side of the house. There was another pool jutting from the second story. It was glassed-in, with a swim-up bar at the farthest end of it.

She stood near the tree line as the many fragrances hit her senses, the faint hint of chlorine from the pools, a top note of rose, and the spicy smell of… Paco Rabanne?

"A drink, Madam?" a male voice asked near her shoulder.

Juliet shook her head without looking at the server. "No, thank you."

An empty drinks platter came at her like a dagger.

"Take a drink, Madam," the man insisted.

Juliet turned around. "All right, Pushy," she told him, lifting her hand–and then stared hard. "Paris!"

"Shh," he told her, glancing over his shoulder.

It was Paris, yes, but he'd shaved his hair to nubs–except the hair on his face. He'd grown that out. And, where'd he get his outfit, the servant's quarters?

Wide-eyed, she charged, "What are you doing here? They all think you're a murderer. Even my own mother believed some of the rumors."

"Italia?" he whispered. "I'm hurt."

Juliet gazed at the guests on the lawn and those walking along the path. "You're going to get caught."

"I won't if you keep your voice down." He lowered his head toward her. "I've been trying to find you."

"You ran from me," she reminded him and hugged her rib with one arm. "*Which* I'm still furious about."

"Because Montague follows your every move," he said, his voice going higher.

She opened her mouth to reply but then was distracted. "Are you wearing contacts?"

He blinked his brown eyes. "They're Portia's."

"Portia's been helping you?"

He nodded.

It was funny how he looked more attractive on the run. *Dios Mio, what do I do with these feelings? Next, I'll be writing to him in Sing-Sing and wanting to marry him.*

Paris said, "Portia was waiting for me the day you came to the house and I hopped the fence. She was in the alley."

"Where is she now?"

"Back at the hotel. No one knows that Portia is in town."

"Em," Juliet said, shifting her weight. "The police might know that she's here. I mentioned it to Nicolo."

He threw out his hand, the one with the empty tray in it. "Why?"

Goodness, it was hard to think with him staring at her, with *brown* eyes. "I- I can't remember right now."

He let the tray fall against his leg. "Well, that's just great."

"Oh, come on. The Novaks probably mentioned Portia's in town, right?"

Paris didn't respond, just stared at her blankly.

She waved her hand as if she shooed a fly away. "Never mind. What do we do now?"

"We prove Noah York killed Jana and Bexley."

Juliet took a step backward. "What makes you so sure he's the murderer?"

"Portia convinced Jana to call off the wedding."

Music floated toward them. The service was about to start. Paris stepped away from her, his eyes squinting as he gazed through the trees at the white chairs and arbor. "Go to your seat. I'll find you again."

"How?"

But Paris already walked away from her, taking a wide berth around the house.

* * *

Juliet sat with her family. It was hard to concentrate on what the chaplain said while Paris roamed the grounds as a drinks server. And, what about his accusation that Noah York killed both Jana and Bexley?

Noah didn't sit with the family, but stood off to the

side of the seating area. He seemed dutifully grief-stricken with his head bowed, and his arms crossed in front of him. He wore a three-piece suit that fit him well. What a striking man, even in sorrow. He'd lift his face once in a while and stare out over the lake. His nose was in perfect proportion to his face, and his dark brows gathered like a storm on the horizon.

It didn't make sense that he killed his *billionaire* fiancé, especially if he'd only been interested in her money. Wouldn't he wait until after the wedding to kill her? Was he as dumb as he was beautiful? *Unless…*

Juliet shifted in her seat and stared across the lake too. *Unless* Jana had broken the engagement on Portia's advice, and Noah killed her in a fit of anger.

But why kill Bexley?

Perhaps Bexley had participated in the murder – and then Noah decided to tie up loose ends–with a balloon string.

Italia poked Juliet in the ribs and nodded toward the dais.

Juliet winced. That was her bad rib.

Italia mouthed: *Pay attention.*

She was paying very close attention, thank you. There wasn't anyone else in the crowd trying to figure out who was the murderer.

Saskia spoke on behalf of the family–and she did it poorly. Her voice was monotone, her features emotionless, and her speech was full of rabbit trails. She spoke more about the rest of the family than about Jana.

Juliet's focus drifted again, out over the lake, and then toward the rose garden on the right. Paris had said he'd find her.

How?

Well, there was nothing else for it. Juliet needed to remain at the Blonde Palace for a while, just to keep Paris from doing something stupid.

* * *

Lunch was served alfresco, and the guests mingled on the patio connected to the house. There were two more pools on the south and west side of the courtyard. Between them were long and short walkways that resembled concrete Popsicle sticks. Alongside the water were giant pots filled with foxtail palms, which defied reason because, hello, this wasn't Florida.

Cyril Novak had designed the home and gardens. He was one of the most sought after architects in the world, according to Juliet's mother. Yet, the real money came from Saskia's family. Saskia's late father owned a conglomerate company that controlled everything from agriculture to real estate.

Again, this was all something Italia had told Juliet. Her mother seemed to idolize the Novak family. Evidently, Italia was going through a midlife crisis. She'd had her hair cut in the Novak's styling salon. It was chin-length now and had finger waves throughout. And, blonde highlights.

She was turning into one of *them*.

Juliet glanced toward the gardens, again with her mouth full of chepalgash, which was some sort of Czech pie with cottage cheese filling … and garlic. She wanted to spit it out, but there was no wastebasket close enough. She still held the cheese pie in her mouth when she saw Hugo Novak.

He stood with a group of his friends on the lawn in front of the roses. And what was that nearby? A chicken?

"The sweetest honey is loathsome in its own deliciousness."

Chapter 6

Juliet swallowed the pie. Why was there a chicken on the lawn? Hugo didn't seem alarmed by it. He wasn't even paying attention to the bird as it pecked near his shoe. No, Hugo focused on the man who stood next to him—the man with ruby red hair, bad skin, and lips the size of Mick Jagger's.

Someone else caught Juliet's eye. A woman walked around the side of one of the pools. Her name was Xenia Novak and she was either Cyril or Saskia's sister, as Juliet recalled. Xenia lived in the Blonde Palace too. She was the one and only brunette in the house. What a rebel. Tall and built like an athlete, Xenia was dressed in a black jacket and slacks. She kept her head down as she moved. Was she reminiscing about Jana?

Juliet moved in the same direction as Xenia, not to meet up with her, but to go into the house–and somehow find Paris.

Suddenly, Xenia said something to a woman near one of the many French doors. "I don't understand why you and Jana were at the Jinlin's Dine-in, Valerie. I like adventure as well as the next person, but that neighborhood is scary."

Valerie was a tall girl, dressed appropriately in black. Had she been with Jana when she died?

She said, "She loved Chinese food."

"I do too. I have it delivered."

Juliet put her hand on the doorknob and balanced herself. She lifted her foot, to adjust her shoe, or to eavesdrop, whichever.

"Jana wanted to go," Valerie said, her voice carrying a note of defensiveness. "She was upset about something and wanted to tell me about it away from the house."

"Upset? She was happy the last time I saw her," Xenia said, her words sharp. "What was she upset about?"

The girl shook her head, her long tresses swinging with the motion. "She never got a chance to say. She went to the ladies' room and never came back to the table."

"It had to be one of the workers. They saw that rock on her finger and killed her for it."

Valerie shrugged. "I think the police ruled out all of the workers. Aren't they looking for some guy who killed another woman the same way, with balloon strings?"

Juliet let her foot drop to the ground and twisted the door handle.

"I don't know anything about the balloons you're talking about, but I know Paris Nobleman." Xenia dropped her shoulders, and her tone softened. "It's not him, I know that. It can't be. He's one of the kindest people I know."

"They probably said the same thing about Ted Bundy," Valerie told her and moved away.

Xenia watched the girl for a moment, but then narrowed her eyes and gazed across the courtyard.

Juliet turned her head and peered in the same direction.

There was Noah York at the bar near one of the pools. Drowning his sorrows, perhaps? Or celebrating?

The only time you celebrate death is when you did the killing, sì?

* * *

Juliet pulled the glass door open and stepped into the large reception area of the house. This was where the Valentine's Ball had played out. Where she stood now, was where Michael Bublé sang on stage that night.

No maze of lemon trees blocked the view, but it wasn't an open marble space either. Corinthian columns lined the room. Beyond them was a bank of wrought iron windows, and above it all were bridges on the second and third stories connecting the two sides of the house.

"You are always beautiful, *ill mio amore*, but I like your hair long."

Juliet recognized her father's voice. Stepping around the massive water fountain in the center of the room, she saw her family near the front door.

Italia stood stiffly, as though there'd been an argument.

Tribly had her hand on the doorknob. She was a shrunken little apple in her black dress. Her eyes went from

Italia to Santos, and then she threw out her hand. "*Basta*! Italia can have her hair cut anyway she likes it."

Italia nodded. "Thank you, *Nonna*." She'd changed from her black dress to a white pantsuit with a shiny purple jacket overtop. Long silver earrings dangled from her ears. *Dios Mio*, she reeked of Saskia Novak.

"I just wished you would've said something," Santos said, holding out his palms and shrugging.

Italia leaned away from him. "I wanted something fresh and new. And Santos, you're not the one who has to style my hair every morning."

"But I am the one who runs my fingers through it, *si*?"

Italia caught sight of Juliet. Stepping forward, she took her by the arm, and pulled Juliet forward. "Tell your father that it's fine to get my hair cut."

"I'm more concerned about your shiny…"

"Never mind," Italia said, dropping her hand. "I suppose you're leaving as well?"

Juliet's attention went from her mother to her father and back again. "Actually, I've decided I'll stay with you this week, *Matri*."

Italia gasped. "Wonderful."

"*Si*, it's phenomenal," Tribly said. Her dark gray eyes landed on her son. "Can we go? I want to put a roast on."

Santos was an elegant man, trim, and broad-shouldered in his black suit. "Why are you staying?" He asked with narrowed eyes. There was a healthy amount of suspicion in his tone.

"I- I want to keep Hugo cheerful."

"No, no." He shook his full head of gray hair. "You want to stick your noses into the murder case."

Santos really wasn't to blame for his bad attitude.

There was a little PTSD in his psyche from Juliet's previous encounters with murderers.

"The Erie police are handling the investigation, *Papa*. Our police have nothing to do with it. I can't just stick my *noses* into anything."

"How do you know the Erie police are involved, eh?" He leaned closer to her, smelling of cedarwood and jasmine.

"I know," she said, speaking slowly, "because we're in Pennsylvania, not New York."

Italia stepped in between them. "Leave her alone, Santos. She wants to stay with Hugo."

"Bad things come in threes, *sì?*" her father said. "*Mia figlia*, she has been involved in two bad things." He moved his head around his wife's and said, "I'm not returning until next week. How will you leave if a killer chases you?"

"I brought my car," she told him, voice climbing. "I can drive away from a killer."

"No. No. You drive over the killer first, and then you come straight home *sì?*" He ignored Juliet then and spun Italia around by the shoulder. "I don't know why you need to stay."

Italia's voice softened. "To be with Saskia."

"It was her niece who died, not her child. Why does she need you?"

Italia glanced around the room. "Santos!"

"My bed will be lonely."

Tribly lifted her voice, "I'm dead over here. I'm dead on the floor. Can we go?"

Italia pushed Santos' hands away. "Go. Go!"

After the door shut behind them, Italia took Juliet's arm, and they walked together toward the first set of stairs.

Her mother stopped abruptly. "I just thought of something. What will you wear all week?"

Juliet faced her. "I'll make a quick trip home and pack a…"

"We have anxious guests," a high-pitched voice said from the other side of the room.

Mali Novak sashayed around the water fountain; she and her constant companion – her camera. Likely she'd filmed the memorial service for her Instagram and Twitter followers. Mali was an Internet Influencer with five hundred thousand fans.

Five hundred thousand!

Yes, that many people turned on their social media sites to listen to Mali's beauty and fashion advice. Juliet had viewed the vlog herself and found it mostly about Mali, Mali, Mali.

Tagging behind her was a tall young woman who was just as blonde as Mali, though hers was a bleach job. It was the three inches of black roots that gave it away. Her name was Teagan, Juliet recalled. She'd seen her in the videos too. There was something about the girl, though, that didn't come across as the type to hold the selfie stick. No, she seemed like someone who liked winged eyeliner, white shirts with black bras, and… peril.

Handing the camera to her friend, Mali faced the lens. "As you know, we're hosting a celebration of life for my cousin, Jana, today, and one of my favorite people is here. Juliet Da Vinci!" She stood close to Juliet and peered at the camcorder. "Juliet? How can I help?"

Juliet glanced at the camera and then at Mali. "I- I didn't bring a suitcase and decided to stay with *Matri* for the week."

"You need clothes?" Mali squealed, hitting a note that only Mariah Carey would understand. "It's makeover time!"

Juliet's mouth took a hard downward turn. "No, I'm fine."

Italia moved aside. "Go on, Juliet, it'll be fun."

Mali had a hold of her arm and pulled Juliet toward the stairs. She turned once and said to her friend, "Get my butt at a good angle."

Teagan hung back two steps.

Someone caught Juliet's eye. One of the servers crossed the marble on the first floor and slipped beneath the stairs.

No, it was Paris.

Juliet's heart beat a new rhythm. Where was her mother…?

Italia had disappeared again.

Mali pulled Juliet up the stairs. "I have lots of clothes we can share. What do you weigh, one hundred pounds, one hundred ten?"

Juliet's jaw dropped. "One twenty-five."

"Oh, sorry," Mali said, remaining on the same step as Juliet. With her hand on one hip, she glanced at Teagan and the camera. "Must be the coat you're wearing. You're just swimming in it." She started up the stairs again. "You should fit into my clothes just fine. If not, we'll fit you with padded bum pants."

The last statement was somewhat lost on Juliet because she was watching for Paris.

Once they were on the second floor bridge, she peered toward the stairs they'd just climbed.

Where is he?

Once across the bridge, they climbed more stairs to the third floor.

There!

Paris was still on the first set of stairs, taking them slowly with his back against the wall.

Juliet lost track of him when they came off the stairs on the third landing.

Mali walked ahead of Juliet and then flung open her bedroom door. "Here we are."

White carpet covered the bedroom floor, and straight across from the entry was a glass island. The bottom of it was ensconced with one inch mirrors all the way around. Leather chairs sat in front of the island, and behind it, were lighted cabinets filled with an array of perfume bottles and makeup tools. The wall curved around toward the closets. *Closets.* Every shelf and cupboard in the wardrobe was lit with accent lighting.

Mali waved her hand at Teagan, and then turned and examined the clothes.

Teagan switched off the camera and slumped in one of the seats at the makeup bar. Was she bored? Juliet would be if all she did was follow someone around and film them. Unless, of course, it was to shoot a television series, like *Game of Thrones* or *The Walking Dead*.

Speaking of the dead, Juliet asked Mali, "How are you doing since Jana died?"

It was Teagan who answered, "Mali doesn't speak unless she's filming. She wants to save her voice." The girl twisted back and forth on the chair. "And she's fine. She and Jana were never close."

"It's still sad, don't you think?"

"Life is sad." Teagan selected a bottle of black nail polish and shook it, making the tiny ball inside rattle. "Mali's psychic told her that the planets have aligned and formed an unlucky path for her."

Juliet let that soak in for a moment. "Jana was the one who died, though."

"Yes," Teagan said, seeming to enjoy the subject. "Mali wasn't surprised by it." Her blue eyes held Juliet's. "What about you? Are you prepared to accept tragedy once in a while?"

"Um, I'm not functioning under a prophecy at present." She bit her lip. "Unless I count Madame Olei's outburst, and all she said was that I'd chase the man I love."

Hmm. Who have I chased recently, besides Paris?

Mali shoved a black catsuit at Juliet and then pulled a pair of thigh-high boots from the closet.

"Oh, I don't think I can wear this," Juliet said, holding up the Lycra suit.

Mali nodded to her friend.

Teagan said, "You won't do it the same justice, but you'll look fine, especially with enhancers."

"Right," Juliet said and placed the boots on the floor.

Mali went through more clothing, ignoring some, pulling out others. She waved at Teagan. "Film us." She handed Juliet an armful of clothing. She gazed behind them. "Don't you work out, Juliet?"

"I don't."

Because I love myself.

Mali's eyes went behind Juliet. "You should at least do something with your glutes." She turned to the camera. "I cannot stress it enough. Work with what you've got, ladies. If you've got nice breasts, show a little skin." She wagged her finger in the air. "Just a little. Nothing slutty."

Mali pulled a flowered mini dress from the closet and piled it on top of the clothes in Juliet's arms. "We'll film you one of the days you're here and dress you properly." Strolling toward the other side of the room, she opened a dresser drawer and tossed Juliet a small bag. "Panties," Mali told her. "Tags still on."

"Take those home with you," Teagan said, and then she gazed in Mali's direction. "Which bedroom?"

"Let's go have a look."

Mali led the way down the hallway–a long way down the hall—with two turns and up a set of three marble steps. "Please make yourself comfortable," she told the camera.

And then the girls left her standing there.

They could've at least opened the door for her, Juliet thought, struggling with the doorknob, and finally pushing the door open. Dumping the pile of clothing on the king size bed, she glanced around the space. The room was half the size of Mali's, which still made it an enormous guest quarter. Wrought iron framed the French doors. Beyond the doors was a narrow balcony with a dinette and chairs.

Juliet stepped outside and looked out over one of the pools. The sky had turned white, and the pool water appeared as cold as the temperature of the air. Turning, she stepped back into her temporary bedroom, noting the fireplace opposite the bed, the chaise, and the rugs on the hardwood flooring. All were in muted colors of charcoal and cream. Behind the bed was a wall of shelving decorated with vases and figurines.

Returning to the bed, she collected the clothing and turned toward the closet. It was a walk-in. Setting the clothes on a chair, she hung the catsuit first.

The sound of the bedroom door opening made her freeze.

Someone hummed.

Paris doesn't hum.

Juliet peeked around the corner of the closet door.

No, it wasn't Paris. It was Cyril Novak who'd stepped into the room. He faced the door and shut it quietly… and then tiptoed toward the bathroom.

Hey!

Well, technically his bathroom, but didn't he have ten others from which to choose? And, he left the door open!

Juliet's chest felt tight. Was he going to …?

The sound of paper crinkling came from inside the bathroom and then the sound of a … lighter.

Cyril was smoking in there?

Okay, that's even worse.

Whatever brand he inhaled smelled like burning trash and molding leaves. Juliet covered her mouth with her hand, refusing to cough. What would happen if she scared the old guy? Why, there was no telling what else he was doing in there besides smoking. He might come running out with his pants down.

Juliet pulled the closet door mostly shut, and waited.

Less than five minutes later, Cyril slipped out of the room.

"Ugh." Juliet waved her hand in front of her nose. "This is not a supper club, sir." Entering the bathroom, which was lovely and extended with a palatial tub, she stepped toward the end of the room and opened a window.

The bedroom doorknob clicked again. Paris hissed, "Juliet?"

Spinning around, she came out of the bathroom with hands on her hips.

He had his hands on his waist, too. "When did you start smoking?"

Juliet grimaced. Her right to smoke was hardly the hot issue. "What do you think you're doing?"

"I got here as fast as I could," he said, his brown eyes wide. "I saw Cyril in the hall and hid behind a rubber plant." He hadn't changed out of the serving coat. The embroidery on the breast pocket read Delectables Catering.

Juliet marched toward him and poked the emblem with her index finger. "I have a lot of questions for you, Paris Nobleman."

"I defy you stars."

Chapter 7

Hey," he said, turning and brushing the embroidery. "I have to return this jacket." He gave her the once over and smiled. "It's good to see you, Juliet. I missed you."

"No, no, no," she told him, wagging her finger. "No flirting. You tell me right-a now what's going on." Okay, yes, she heard it that time; her father's tone had come out of her mouth.

Sue me. I'm Italian.

Paris let out a long breath and sat on the chaise lounge. "Ask me anything."

Narrowing her eyes, she stepped toward him. "Why

are you so casual about this situation?"

He shrugged. His scruffy beard moved with the downward turn of his mouth. "I have the best private detective on the case, yeah?"

She tilted her head and shook it at the same time. He'd hired a detective? "Who?"

"You, of course."

She gasped. "You can't trust me. All I'm good for are wild guesses and panic." Covering her heart with her hand, Juliet admitted, "Mostly panic."

He sat there, unfazed. "You said you have questions."

"Questions, yes." She paced a moment, but quickly spun around. "What happened to Bexley Pemberton-Kerr? Why were you in a hotel room with her? How did she die?"

Paris held up both hands to stop the flow.

Juliet didn't stop. "And tell me why you ran away from the scene. You look guilty. If I was an officer, I'd arrest you."

"Okay, okay. I ran away from the hotel room because the crazy Spanish maid kept shouting *murderer, murderer.*" Placing his hands on his knees, he tucked one foot beneath the chaise, and leaned forward. "I had to think of my sister. Noah will try to kill Portia because she's the one who talked Jana out of marrying him. I was trying to protect her."

"First things first. The maid was Italian."

He raised and lowered his brows. "That explains all the screaming."

Juliet's hands landed on her hips again. "So, you've assumed that Noah killed Bexley and Jana, and that Portia is next on his list?"

"Remember the last time I spoke to you, and I had to get off the phone? It was Bexley. She was in a panic.

Said she'd witnessed Jana's murder and had run from the scene." He pushed to his feet. "She knew the police would blame her for the murder because she'd been following Noah and Jana around. They'd issued a restraining order."

"But, why would Bexley call you, Paris?"

"We dated," he admitted in a slower tone than usual.

He met someone… but Bexley? Come on!

Paris seemed to read her thoughts and said, "It was way over a year ago, Juliet. Bexley's mother threw her at me in the same manner that Italia threw you at me." Taking a long breath, he rubbed the short hair on his head a couple of times. "My mother and Mrs. Kerr thought Bexley and I would hit it off. And, we did … I did anyway. Bexley was beautiful and adventurous." He grinned at Juliet. "I have a type, yeah?"

She leaned away from him. "Are you seriously comparing me to a stalker?"

His eyes lifted above her head for a second and then came back to hers. "I didn't know she was a stalker back then."

"Right," Juliet said, rolling her hand. "So, what happened?"

His mouth turned down at the corners. "Bexley didn't love me. She was already in love with Noah York. The Pemberton-Kerrs didn't approve of Noah, so Bexley pretended to love me and met Noah on the side."

Juliet's shoulders sagged, and she sank down on the chaise. "Oh." She remembered him saying he'd never love someone again that didn't love him back. Now she knew why. "This all happened in Martha's Vineyard, right?"

"Yeah. Once Bexley's parents discovered the deception, they got rid of Noah by circulating the truth that he's a money grabbing gold digger to all their friends." Paris took a seat beside her. "Noah left town, moved out here, and Bexley followed him. I thought they were still together until Noah proposed to Jana Novak."

"So, Bexley called you in a panic?"

He nodded. "Right."

"She saw Noah kill Jana?"

Paris held her eyes and shook his head. "No, she didn't say it was Noah. She got off the phone once she asked for help. By the time I reached her hotel room, she was already dead."

Juliet put her hands behind her and leaned there, thinking it through. "How'd you get into the hotel room, if she was dead?"

"She wasn't answering her phone, so I borrowed the housekeeper's key and…" He stared off toward the closet area. "I was too late."

Juliet stuck her legs out in front of her and eyed her boots. She crossed them and re-crossed them. "This is bad, Paris."

"I know."

"It would've been helpful if Bexley had told you what she saw."

"I know."

"And then left a detailed message of how she died, you know? Followed by a lengthy description of the killer."

"A lengthy description of Noah York," Paris said, head bobbing.

"Well, we need to prove it, Paris."

A smile broke through the scruff. "I know you'll figure out how to catch Noah."

"It may not have been Noah. It could've been someone

at the Jinlin's Dine-In"

"Jin, what?"

"Jinlin's. It's where Jana died." She bit her thumb cuticle for a moment, thinking again. "Bexley was stalking Noah and Jana. Why? Was she trying to scare Jana?" She dropped her hand to her lap. "Maybe it *was* Noah who killed her."

"I told you!"

Juliet let out a long breath. "We should examine Noah's bedroom. See if he has any alley dust on his clothes, any balloon ties lying around. But, how do we know which one is his bedroom?"

"He's been staying in the cottage out back," Paris said, getting off the chaise and walking toward the window by the bed. "It's not visible from here, it's around the corner."

"I imagine he'll be moving out soon, now that Jana's gone. We'll need to work fast."

"Oh, I don't think he'll leave. He's in here now. He'll go for one of the other ladies."

"Okay, ew," Juliet told him and sat forward. "The first thing we do is to find evidence that he's the killer, and then we go from there."

"After dark?"

She nodded. "After dark. Until then, hide in here, but not in the bathroom. I seem to attract visitors there."

* * *

Dinner was at seven o'clock in a dining room with seating for twelve. Three sets of wrought iron doors overlooked another patio, which faced westward. The pink fingers of the sun held onto the horizon for all they were worth.

Italia sat with the Novaks at one end of the table, wearing a new outfit. It was a matching top and skirt of vintage roses on cream. She looked stunning in it. The skin on her toned arms was dusky-hued, and Italia's newly blonde highlighted hair glistened in the chandelier light. My, how she fits in with the Novaks. Notice how, with such ease, she laughs with Saskia and semi-flirts with Cyril.

I'm going to need to do an intervention soon, aren't I?

Juliet ate at the other end of the table. Mali and Teagan made a brief appearance, saw the starchy food, and decided not to eat. Hugo remained at Juliet's side, but so did his friend, Gerald.

Gerald was the ruby-haired fellow who Juliet had seen earlier in the day. Mick Jagger's lips and a bad attitude was what Gerald brought to the table.

"Where is Noah?" Juliet asked Hugo. "Doesn't he come to the table with the family?"

Hugo had his head down, and he threw a glance at Gerald. "He's busy tonight."

Juliet turned to Gerald.

Gerald wore a big smirk on his big lips. "Yeah, busy."

Juliet stopped her fork midway to her mouth. "Does that mean he's out for the evening?"

"Stop worrying about Noah," Hugo told her. "You're going to marry me, remember?" He shot a look down the table at his mother.

"Oh ... right," Juliet said, and took a bite of braised beef. "But, is he out for the evening?"

Hugo narrowed his pale eyes. "I don't know. I only know he's not here now." He laughed again and glanced at Gerald.

Right.

"May I take my plate to my room to finish?" she asked, covering it with her napkin.

Hugo frowned. "I guess."

"Thanks," she told him and got to her feet.

* * *

Paris ate the remainder of what was on Juliet's plate and then wiped his mouth with a napkin. "It's getting dark. We can cross the lawn and check Noah's cottage."

"He could be in his room. All Hugo said was that Noah was *busy*."

"We have to do it sometime." Paris stood and set the plate on the dresser near the French doors.

Juliet opened the door and stepped onto the balcony.

Gerald and Hugo sat in chairs beside the pool. Both wore sweaters and jeans and held cans of beer in their hands.

Back inside, Juliet checked the window overlooking the lawn. Floodlights lit the center garden, and uplighting hit the ferns. "You should stay here," Juliet said. "The family is still downstairs."

Paris shook his head. "You don't know what to look for."

"Of course I do," she told him, letting the curtain fall into place again. "Balloon strings and the whiff of a Chinese restaurant on his clothing. Maybe a memento from the Porta di Messa Hotel."

He stared at her blankly. "The engagement ring is what we should look for, Juliet." He wrinkled his brow. "The whiff of a Chinese … is this what I can expect from you as my detective?"

"Maybe you should pay me more," she told him, opening the closet door and grabbing a black sweater. She turned back around and then jerked to a stop.

Paris blocked the exit. "Would you like me to pay you now?" His hand reached for her waist.

She batted his hands away. "Knock it off. This is serious business." She scooted around him. "And I'm not your detective."

He made an inarticulate sound, and then, "Fine."

"Why do you think Noah has the ring?" she asked, heading for the door and then spinning around to wait for him.

Paris was still in the closet, pulling a large sweater off a hanger. "The ring was missing when they found Jana. That's what Mali told Portia before Portia hightailed it out of here to find me." He pulled the sweater over his head and rolled it down over his white shirt. It was a snug fit. "I don't think Noah bought the ring. I think Jana did and I think it's Noah's ticket out. If he can't woo another billionaire, he'll sell it for a ton of money."

She twisted the doorknob. "You're going to stretch that sweater out of shape, and it's not mine. I have to give that back to Mali."

"She'll live," Paris said, approaching and then bringing his face close to Juliet's, as though he meant to kiss her. "I'm sure Mali didn't give you her favorite things."

Juliet stepped aside, opened the door–and thwacked Paris on the forehead with it. "Let's go."

Paris mouthed the word *ouch*, rubbed his forehead, and then he followed her out of the room.

All was quiet on the third floor. Mali's bedroom door was closed, and Juliet and Paris made it to the second story landing without incident … until the parrot in a cage on a stand saw them and let out a high C, able-to-break-glass squuuuaaawwwk that only the jungles of the ancient Waipoua Forest had previously heard.

It went right up Juliet's spine. The noise went out of her ears instead of in.

Paris squatted. For some unknown reason he just squatted right there on the landing. Maybe it was his way of holding in his terror? But then he jumped up immediately afterward, grabbed Juliet's hand, and raced for the patio doors at the end of the landing.

Cement stairs took them to the courtyard and gardens. They ran along the tree line, staying out of the lighting.

Once Paris dropped Juliet's hand, she rubbed the spot above her left breast. "My heart still hurts."

"It was just a bird, Juliet. Pull yourself together."

"You have no reason to correct me, Squatting Man."

He kept going, but said over his shoulder, "It was either squat or fall over dead from fright."

"Right. Watch the chicken …"

"Damn the chicken and damn the bird."

Juliet frowned. Someone had a tone. "Why do the Novaks own chickens anyway?" she asked, keeping in step with Paris. "This isn't exactly a farm."

"You know Cyril, always coming up with something quirky."

A chicken coop was off to the right of the path. It was a pretty little place with fencing all around it and flower box windows. There was a door, too. A wide open door for the chicken to come and go as they liked.

Paris circled the coop and then changed directions, back toward the eastern side of the house.

Juliet finally saw it, a cottage attached to the main house. "That's Noah's cottage? Why doesn't he stay in the main house?"

Paris whispered, "Privacy, I guess."

Two cement steps led to a wooden front door. White string lights framed the pair of windows on either side of the door.

Juliet climbed the steps and knocked.

Paris threw out his hands and glared at her. "Why?"

The house was quiet. Juliet waited and then pulled a credit card from her bra. "Always knock before breaking and entering…" She peered at Paris in the twinkle lights. "You do want to do this while he's not home, right?"

Paris didn't answer; he just stared at her.

She stuck the card between the door and the jamb, jiggled the card, and then opened the door.

It was a speed record for her.

Peeking around the wood, she checked the room. "All clear."

Noah had left a light on in the loft area in the back of the cottage. Beyond the front living area was a small kitchen, and farther back was another door. A bathroom was on the other side of the kitchen, and between them was a spiral staircase made of coarse cement. The place had probably been a gardener's cottage at one time.

Juliet moved toward the kitchen bar separating the living space. A travel brochure lay there. "Australia," Juliet read aloud. "You said he was an adventurer?"

"Professional, according to him."

"Right," Juliet said, moving the brochure and studying the paper beneath it. There were notes, handwritten, and a list of items to purchase—or so it seemed.

"Where would he hide the ring?" Paris asked with hands on his waist.

"Check upstairs."

"Right," he said and climbed the steps.

Juliet went around the bar and gazed into the trashcan. There was an empty box of noodles and a banana skin inside. Unless Noah York used the banana peel as a slipping device as he strangled his victims, there was nothing in the pail to arouse suspicion.

She moved to the bathroom next and opened the medicine cabinet. Allergy meds, Tylenol, and a tube of some kind of ointment…

Oh, but what do we have here?

Juliet picked up an unmarked pill bottle and opened it. Inside were triangular pills, turquoise in color. "You look perfectly illegal." She set them back in the cabinet.

The outside door opened and a light in the front room switched on.

"Some consequence yet hanging in the stars."

Chapter 8

Juliet's eyes almost popped out of their sockets.

Shutting the medicine cabinet, she stepped toward the doorframe, and leaned, looking out the doorway.

The smell of vodka hit her nose. Not just a hint of it either, but a big whiff as though she'd leaned over a barrel and snorted half of it.

The refrigerator door opened, and a dull light emanated from the kitchen.

Juliet slipped carefully into the middle of the front room and peeped into the kitchen.

Noah had his head practically inside the refrigerator

and his forearm on the door.

Lifting her chin, she glanced into the loft.

Paris stood at the railing. He mouthed, "Distract him."

"How?" she mouthed right back.

He leaned forward and batted his eyes and puckered his lips.

Juliet shook her head and motioned, "You do it."

The refrigerator door slammed shut, making the bottles inside rattle. Without looking around, Noah twisted the top off a beer and took a long swig.

Juliet held her breath, backed toward the door, and then opened it and slammed it shut.

Noah spit his beer all over the kitchen cabinets.

"Oh," Juliet said. "I'm so sorry. I thought this was the pool house."

Wiping his mouth with the back of his hand, Noah took a step forward. "Damn, you scared me." He weaved a little as he came around the kitchen island.

Noah was taller than Juliet had first guessed. He was at least six foot two and lean muscled. He wore a muted striped shirt and blue jeans. The sleeves were rolled up, revealing his tattooed forearms. "Where's your bikini?"

She returned his stare with a question forming on her lips.

"You said you were going swimming."

Oh right!

"I thought I'd find one in here to borrow." She stared over his shoulder.

Paris was halfway down the spiral staircase.

Noah's light-colored eyes took in Juliet again, and he stepped closer, grinning like the wolf from Red Riding Hood. "It's too cold to swim, unless we go skinny dipping together. What did you say your name is?"

"Juliet Da Vinci," she said and cleared her throat. "I came to the memorial service."

Paris was off the bottom of the steps now, tiptoeing backward to the kitchen door.

She dragged her eyes back to Noah's. "I'm sorry for your loss."

"You're beautiful," Noah told her, moving toward the coffee table and taking a glass from a tray on a nearby table.

Juliet said, "So are you."

Paris frowned and held up the palms of his hands.

She shrugged and shook her head.

Noah poured a small amount of beer into the glass and then held it out for Juliet.

"No, thank you."

"Da Vinci … Da Vinci," he said, tilting his head. "I know that name."

"Leonardo?"

He threw back his head and laughed. Sobering, he pointed his finger. "Wines. Are you part of the wine family?"

"Yes," she answered, stealing a glance into the kitchen.

Paris had his hand on the doorknob.

"Well, well, rich and pretty," Noah said, setting the glass aside. "You're a catch."

She backed toward the front door, ready to exit as soon as Paris made his move. "Already caught," she told Noah, hand on the doorknob.

"Really?" he said, weaving a little. "I didn't see a ring on your finger … and I looked."

"But my heart is taken."

"A woman's heart is fickle, Juliet. It can change its mind

many times. What is your love's name?"

Paris opened the back door. A squeaking noise came from the hinges of it.

Noah started to turn around.

Juliet shouted, "Paris Nobleman! I'm in love with Paris Nobleman."

Noah whipped back around.

Juliet shot a look at Paris.

He stood utterly still, but he grinned at Juliet as though she spoke the truth.

Idiot.

Noah pointed his chin at the ceiling and said, "Oh, no! No, no, no. Paris Nobleman, the *yeah* guy?"

Juliet squared her shoulders. "It's reflexive and charming."

"It's not," Noah argued. He took a step toward her. "I owe it to you to change your heart's mind about him."

Juliet twisted the knob, ready to pull on the door. "So, you know Paris?"

He lifted his beer bottle in salute. "He's a gullible fool."

Juliet narrowed her eyes. A drop of acid formed in her stomach. She was the only one who was allowed to speak about Paris in that manner. "He's amazing, and he's loyal, and funny …"

"I accept," Noah told her.

"Accept what?"

"The challenge to win your heart."

Wide-eyed, Juliet said, "Oh my goodness." She stared at the back door. "Is that Jana?"

Noah jerked backward, as though she'd slapped him. He spun around hard toward the kitchen.

Paris pulled the door open and ran.

Juliet did the same, out the front door.

She didn't wait for Paris to catch up with her. Juliet skirted the chicken coop and then raced up the outside stairs to the second floor. She only slowed when she reached the birdcage.

Fool me once little birdie…

Someone had covered the birdcage with a black cloth. But the bird still made noise by scratching and whistling.

Juliet crept slowly past it and then shot toward her room in a mad dash. Whipping off her coat, she tossed it into the closet without hanging it up, and then she fell into a reading chair near the bed.

Paris was a minute behind her and slipped into the room noiselessly. He sat on the edge of the bed and leaned toward her. "I think Noah saw me. Thank you for pointing me out."

She waved him off. "He was too drunk to recognize you."

"Do you see how quickly he came on to you? He wasn't in love with Jana." He put both hands on the bottom of the sweater and then tugged it over his head.

"But, why would he kill them, Paris? If Jana broke up with him, why not try to talk her into marrying him again. I mean he's ridiculously handsome. He could talk anybody into anything."

Paris rolled the sweater into a ball. "Even you?"

"Of course not."

"You said, anybody."

"I also said that my heart was taken."

"Yes, you did." His mouth lifted at the corners.

"I lie too easily these days," she said, lifting her thumb to her mouth, ready to chew a cuticle. Before she did, though, "I should go see Father Jonathan and confess."

Paris lost his smile. "Right."

"We need to study the alley where Jana was murdered. That's our next step."

He got off the bed, taking the sweater with him. "My next step is going to sleep."

Juliet got out of the chair and followed him. "Where are you sleeping?"

"Right here," he told her, waving at the bed.

She stopped abruptly. "That's my bed."

"You're going to be that way, yeah?"

"Yeah."

He opened the closet door and tossed the sweater inside. "I'll take the chaise." He unbuttoned his white shirt and moved toward the bathroom. "First, a shower."

A shower? That was a teensy intimate, wasn't it? Sure, Paris had lived at the vineyard for months, but there were no bedroom visits, and no showering in the same bathroom.

Going to the closet, Juliet searched for a pair of pajamas. Had Mali shared? Never mind, she'd wear the ugly striped leggings and the long gray sweater with the peekaboo shoulders. Tying up her hair, she waited for Paris on the edge of the bed.

Paris strolled out of the steamy bathroom in a pair of boxers.

"Paris Nobleman," Juliet said, pushing off the bed. "Where are your pants?"

He had a hair-free chest, thank God. Juliet didn't know what she'd do if he was curly all over—probably run screaming from the room. He had very rippled chest muscles though, and defined arms. His skin was a nice color and not pasty like a fish.

Yes, he's attractive. And he'd better stop it right now.

She turned her face away. "There are sheets on the shelf in the closet."

"All right, Prissy," he said and turned away.

Juliet climbed into bed and snapped off the lamp, leaving him in the dark.

"Do you mind?" he asked, finding a light switch.

That made the situation worse. Now Juliet had a view of him in the light. It was like watching a movie with Paris as the half-naked star.

Why is he so attractive?

Angry, Juliet stood and dragged the comforter from the bed. She and the quilt went for a walk onto the balcony. Once there, she sat on a lounger and arranged the blanket around her legs.

There would come a time when she'd need to figure out how she felt about Paris. Juliet had not forgotten his kiss at the Valentine Ball, nor the way she missed him while she'd been in Italy.

Am I ready to say the L word again?

A tiny spark of fear settled in her stomach. Commitment, Tribly had said. Was Juliet ready to commit her heart to Paris Nobleman?

She gazed out over the pool and the dark spikes of the evergreen trees beyond the water. No one was outside, and the only sound came from the waterfall somewhere around the bend of the house. The pool water rippled and made the lights beneath the surface wavy. Funny, it didn't seem as cold on the balcony as it did when she'd crossed the lawn earlier.

Was Paris right about Noah York, that he was the murderer? Juliet wasn't sure, because there were plenty of other people who could've killed Jana and Bexley. Take Hugo's friend, Gerald. He looked like a type of guy who took delight in balloons. He was a clown with his red hair and big lips.

And, what about Teagan, Mali's friend? She could've killed the women. Teagan liked her black nail polish a little too much for someone who had zero interest in murder.

Juliet pulled the blanket to her chin.

The only thing that seemed absolute was that Bexley was murdered because she saw someone kill Jana. That meant Bexley's killing was an afterthought.

But whoever killed Jana had a motive, *sì*.

Noah might've had a motive, but did Gerald, or Teagan? What about Saskia? She seemed capable of murder. It was easy to come up with a mental picture of her holding a balloon string taut in one hand while drinking a glass of bubbly with the other.

Everyone needed a lot more studying before Juliet would be as confident as Paris was about who had murdered the ladies.

An hour later, she trudged back into the room, pulling the comforter with her. The fatness of the blanket clogged the doorway, and she needed to grab the edges with two hands to haul it inside again.

All the lights were off in the room—except the fire in the hearth. Soft breathing came from the chaise area.

Juliet crept toward Paris, just to make sure he was asleep. "Paris?"

He didn't answer.

"Good night," she said and turned toward the bed.

* * *

The sun in her face woke Juliet at eight-thirty.

Paris had awakened first and stood near the French doors where the sunshine streamed into the room. He was already dressed in his black pants and white shirt.

Juliet sat up against the pillows. "You look as though you're going somewhere."

Paris turned and came toward the bed. He'd removed the contacts, and his eyes were bright green again. "I'm going to wait for you outside the gates."

"How are you going to get out of here?"

He lifted one shoulder. "The same way I got in. Meet me at the gate?"

"I have to shower and make an appearance downstairs first." She pushed the covers off her legs. "I'll need an excuse to leave."

"All right," he said, getting off the mattress. "I'll see you out there."

"Be careful."

"Are you worried?" he asked at the door.

"No," she lied and walked into the bathroom. That'd teach him to be so gorgeous all the time.

Juliet showered and dressed in loose-fitting blue jeans, yes, loose in the butt area, a teal top, and a dark green jacket. She made it downstairs by nine thirty.

There was a lineup of food on the extensive buffet at the front of the room. Juliet bypassed it and went straight to the coffee pot at the far end of the table. The three sets of glass doors looked out over the lawn and gardens. There was no sign of Paris, so Juliet selected a blue china cup from a tray and reached for the glass coffee carafe.

Dear God, what was inside of it? It smelled a little bit like coffee, but why was it so murky? Had someone already added milk? And, where was the espresso machine? These people could afford an espresso machine–they could afford a Wake-Up Café too. Install it right outside the kitchen with employees and coffee cakes.

Okay, she needed to calm down.

The Wake-Up Café was only a forty-five minute drive. That was a spot Juliet needed to hit before exploring dark alleys of Erie with Paris.

Taking a breath, Juliet spun around.

Noah York blocked her way. He dipped his head and leaned in. "That was a terrible thing you did last night."

Her stomach knotted.

Noah stood too close, and he smelled like Old Spice shower soap and brandy. His dark green eyes twinkled in the recessed lighting. "Bringing up my dead fiancé was cruel."

Juliet swallowed hard, feeling the heat rise to her cheeks. "I didn't think you'd remember. You were pretty drunk."

"And you're spunky." He bent nearer, bringing his face closer and closer. "I like you."

Someone cleared their throat behind him.

Noah spun on his heel.

Xenia stood there, tall and disapproving. She wore green combat pants, hiking boots, and a black sweater with a wolf printed on the front.

Has Mali seen her dressed like that; why wasn't it makeover time for Xenia?

Xenia was in her late thirties, and quite severe-looking, like a public school teacher who'd been at it too long. She asked, "Still drinking, Noah?"

He left the room, taking the coffee pot with him. "Only to forget, dear Xenia."

Xenia gazed at Juliet. "I'm sorry. I hope he wasn't bothering you." She moved around Juliet and took a breakfast plate from the buffet.

"Actually, your timing was perfect."

"He needs to go. My sister-in-law allows him to stay and grieve." Picking up a spoon, she dropped scrambled egg on the plate. "Noah is taking advantage of the situation."

Juliet slid closer to her, with her back to the cabinetry. "You don't think he's grieving?"

The woman shook her head. There was no softness about her at all. "I don't know what to think. I know I'm shattered over my niece's death, but Noah doesn't seem to feel the same way." She moved on and ladled mixed fruit onto her plate. "He did play the girls against each other. Maybe he thinks he can talk Mali into marrying him."

"Really?" Juliet frowned. "I didn't think Mali was interested in Noah."

"You should pay more attention then," Xenia said and moved toward the toaster.

* * *

Juliet's car was still parked in the gravel on the easternmost side of the house. Tossing her purse on the passenger seat, she pulled the Fiat around toward the blacktop road that led to the front gates. Something to her left caught her attention.

There was a glassed-in garage jutting from the bottom floor of one of the wings of the house. Vintage cars had been parked up on platforms with pendant lights shining on the high gloss paint jobs and fenders. It looked like a museum.

Turning left, Juliet took the long drive through the pine forest, watching for Paris as she went. Had he had time to get to the gate? She supposed it depended on whether or not he needed to dodge security cameras.

There was the bridge straight ahead and Juliet slowed.

Suddenly, the passenger side door opened, and Paris jumped into the front seat. "Go, go, go. There are cameras on the bridge."

Juliet hit the gas.

* * *

After stopping for coffee, Juliet drove toward the part of Erie that needed some attention from the city council. Paris sat straighter, reached past her shoulder, and locked the door. Then he locked his own.

"What is that?" Juliet asked, turning the wheel and avoiding something in the center of the road.

"Metal sheeting," he told her, bracing his hands on the dash.

"Have I accidentally driven into Pakistan?" she asked, coming to a red light and braking the car.

"Don't stop!"

Juliet waved her hand over the steering wheel. "There's a light…"

"That's just someone's ploy to rob you. Turn here." He held her phone and studied the display. "The Dine-In is up here on the right."

A black Pontiac passed them on the left. There was no passenger-side door, and the driver's seat was an overturned bucket.

It was somewhat distracting.

When Juliet glanced right again, she saw a red and white sign with the words Jinlin's Dine-In, and an arrow pointing into a parking area.

"Drive around to the alley."

"Right, right," she said, turning the wheel again. "Look at the bus stop. That's quite a crowd. Wait, is that a duck on that man's head?"

Paris rubbed his thighs with the palms of his hands. "Head warmer by day, dinner by night."

"Aww, I thought it was a pet duck." She drove into the road again and then into the unpaved alley. Three dumpsters sat behind the strip center, some with trash falling over the sides of them. An empty wheelchair was parked next to one of them. Across the alley was a forested area from which a man emerged, zipping his trousers.

Overall it was a vast improvement to the front side of the building.

"Watch the pothole," Paris said, holding onto the dash. "Watch the child…"

"That's not a child," Juliet said, hitting brakes and watching the man cross to the trees. "That's a gang member."

"He's underage." He sat back in his seat again and adjusted the seatbelt over his chest. "He reminds me of your friend, Abram, except with more tattoos."

Juliet slowed. "I cannot imagine Jana coming here to eat. I don't care how authentic the food is."

"Well, you know the Novaks. Everyone is an adventurer."

Juliet nodded. "Except Hugo."

"Hugo again. Has he tried to kiss you?"

"He's gay, Paris. Catch on."

He leaned away from her, making the seat crackle.

"Then why did he kiss you?"

"To fool his mother." She pulled even with a dumpster that had balloons hanging out of the top of it and put the car into Park. "Here it is, the scene of the crime."

Paris sat forward, gazing at the dumpster. "I never told you that Bexley had a balloon tied around her neck. Did Nicolo tell you?"

"I have *the gift…*" she said, using Tribly's fortune telling voice.

"No, you don't. Nicolo told you."

Juliet ignored him and gazed at the door near the dumpster. A small placard near the door read, Yumi Flowers. She slipped the car into Drive again.

Now, what had Paris been talking about again?

Oh, yes. Nicolo.

"Officer Montague didn't tell me anything. He said it was a confidential police matter, and all of that." She drove to the front of the stores again and parked.

"How did you find out, yeah?"

"The same way I'm going to find out what happened to Jana… yeah?" She wiggled her eyebrows at him.

Paris' mouth parted and his eyes narrowed into little slits. "I'm scared now."

Yumi Flowers was next door to Jinlin's. Exotic Flowers, the sign claimed.

It looked ordinary to Juliet, less than ordinary, really. If it was so exotic, what were the balloons and party favors doing on sale for fifty cents? The outside of the place was just as derelict as the other stores in the strip mall. Maybe the exotic stuff–the drugs, counterfeit and fake ID maker–were hidden behind that barred door over there. They walked inside.

An Asian man stood at a table behind the glass counter,

paying no attention to them, and arranging stems in a vase. He was older, maybe fifty, and he wore his hair long to his tee-shirt collar. Gray hair marked his temples, and goatee. When he finally looked up, he bowed his head again, and then, "May I help you?"

Aww, he seems nice.

Juliet stepped closer to the glass case. "*Nihao*," she said.

"*Konnichiwa*," the man said in return and bowed again.

"Oh, you're Japanese. *Konnichiwa*."

"I speak English better than Japanese," he told her, leaving the bouquet and stepping toward the counter. "How may I help you?"

"I'm looking for a balloon …"

He waved his hand above him. "All around you, *hai*. Which one would you like?"

And then Juliet saw, above the refrigerator cases, flattened balloons tacked to the wall. "Sorry, none of those. I'm looking for a kiss balloon, like big lips. All I see are rabbits and eggs."

"Well, it's Easter, lady."

Aww, he seems mean.

She leaned away from the counter. "You can't love someone on Easter?"

He jabbed his pruning scissors toward the wall. "There is a heart balloon."

"I want a kiss. I saw one here last week or the week before."

"Last week, *hai*, but they were leftover from Valentine in February. It was time to toss them."

"In the dumpster out back?"

"*Hai*," he said, almost absently, but then he stared at her with just a hint of suspicion. He stood straighter.

"Who are you?"

Juliet set her hands on the counter and tapped her fingernails on the glass. "I'm investigator DaVinci."

A funny noise escaped Paris and he moved away.

Undeterred, she said, "I was hired by the Novaks to follow up on the murder of Jana Novak with one of *your* balloons."

"No, no, no," Yumi said, snapping the pruning shears to emphasize his words. "I don't own the balloons when they go into the trash. They are the city's balloons. Mr. Erie himself owns them. Go talk to him."

Juliet wrinkled her forehead. "No, they are your balloons until the garbage man collects them." She stopped tapping her nails. "But, the Novaks aren't suing you, so relax."

His eyes got big. "Do not tell me to relax when you accuse my balloons of murder."

"Then tell your balloons to stop hanging out of the dumpster so they won't become murder weapons."

He stepped away from the counter. "What do you want?"

Juliet relaxed her shoulders. "You were in the alley the day of the murder because you'd thrown balloons away." She was guessing again, fishing … dumpster diving as 'twere.

He gave her a jerky nod.

"Did you hear anything?"

His eyes tracked the ceiling. "The usual arguing that comes from the kitchen."

"Arguing? What about?"

"How should I know?"

She pursed her lips, thinking. "Jinlin's, is that Chinese or Japanese food?"

"Chinese."

"You don't speak Chinese?"

"I don't know Chinese, but I do know the Korean language. It is similar to Japanese." He pointed his shears toward the wall. "The men there speak Korean."

"Oh," Juliet let out. "Well, what did they say?" she asked, forgetting to be the hardboiled PI she was going for here.

"They hate the owner. He doesn't pay enough."

"Oh," she repeated, but less enthusiastically. "Did they say anything strange, like *what are you doing?*" What Juliet had in mind was the statement Jana's girlfriend said to Xenia, that Jana went to the restroom and never came back to the table. Had she gone to the kitchen, flashing the ring, and one of the cooks thought to rob her?

Mr. Yumi shook his head. "No, only the usual whining that Koreans do."

So, we're going racist.

"Did you see anyone else in the alley?"

"A woman. That's what I told the police. Why don't you talk to them?"

"What did she look like?"

"Tall, blonde, wearing a red blouse."

"Bexley," Paris said. He leaned against the refrigerated case with his hands in his pockets.

Juliet turned back to Yumi. "What was she doing?"

"Watching the alley from the trees."

"Stalking," Juliet summarized. "Did you see her leave?"

He approached the counter and took one flower from the vase. "I was back inside, but I heard a car leave. The tires squealed."

"You only heard one car?"

"I *heard* only one car. It left from the front parking lot. And I saw another car leave the alley."

Juliet frowned. "You heard a car squeal out of the front parking lot, but then saw a car leave the alley?"

"*Hai.*"

"Bexley pulled out of the front parking lot," Paris put in.

Juliet nodded. "So the car pulling out of the alley, was…" She looked at Yumi again. "What did the second car look like?"

He chopped a bit off the stem of the rose. "It was old, blue-green, boxy."

"Noah," Paris added.

Juliet frowned at him. "Quit guessing."

He shrugged. "Fine. You keep guessing then."

She faced Yumi again. "When did you find out that someone had died in the alley?"

"When the police came." He nodded to someone behind Juliet, and said, "Hello detective."

Juliet turned around.

"Tis an ill cook that cannot lick his own fingers."

Chapter 9

A man stood off to the right, chewing gum. He had a pointy chin and tapered nose, like a hawk.

Paris had somehow magically disappeared. Was he crouching in an aisle somewhere?

Yumi waved his hand toward Juliet. "Do you two know each other?"

The hawk raised his brows. "Should we know each other?" He bit down hard on his gum, making it snap loudly.

Juliet stuck out her hand. "Private Investigator Da Vinci."

The man tucked his chin. "Da Vinci? Juliet Da Vinci?" His lips disappeared into a thin smile. "Nicolo told me all about you." He didn't take her offered hand.

Juliet dropped her arm to her side. "He hasn't told me anything about you."

"My name is Detective Adams. Where's Paris Nobleman?"

He got right to it, didn't he?

She lifted a shoulder. "I'm looking for him too."

"You came in with someone," Mr. Yumi added.

Now he's helpful?

"When?" Juliet challenged, narrowing her eyes on the guy.

Yumi waved his pruners toward the door. "When you came in."

Adams swooped out of the store and stood on the sidewalk out front.

Juliet held up her index finger. "You've got a bad Yelp review coming, Pal."

Outside on the sidewalk, she peered at the bus stop. Was Paris hiding in plain sight, or had he disappeared into one of the shops?

Gum popped near Juliet's ear, and she turned.

Adams' dark hair lay flat on his head, except for a cowlick on the left side. "Why are you here, Miss Da Vinci?"

Juliet decided to keep it aboveboard with the detective. "I was going to buy a balloon, but Mr. Yumi didn't have what I was looking for."

"Is that right?"

"Absolutely."

He considered her for a moment, tilting his head and

squinting his eyes. "Montague warned me you'd snoop around."

"Did he?"

"He told me not to believe anything you said."

Juliet pressed her lips together and reached into her purse for her cell phone. She hit Nicolo's number.

"Yeah, you two work it out," Adams said in a bored tone and then retraced his steps to the florist's shop.

Nicolo said, "Hello," in a terse tone.

Juliet stared at the sidewalk while she spoke. "Did you tell Detective Adams not to believe anything I said?"

"Where are you?"

"You don't trust me?" Juliet switched the phone to her other ear.

Nicolo made a strangled sound on the other end. "Not particularly. Not when you're in your snooping mode anyway. Where'd you meet Adams?"

"In a flower shop." Juliet stepped off the sidewalk and stood next to the Fiat. She glanced around the parking lot. No sign of Paris anywhere…

"The one next door to Jinlin's?"

Her eyes went to the front of the restaurant, and its red-painted door with symbols above it. "It's a funny name for a restaurant, isn't it?"

"You're investigating again."

"I just happened to be driving by, Nicolo. I saw a guy with a duck on his head." She opened the car and sat in the seat without closing the door.

"Were you hustling the florist?"

Her mouth turned downward. "Hustling?" That sounded as though she walked the streets.

"Did you lie about who you were?"

Detective Adams pushed open the door and stepped onto the sidewalk again. He watched Juliet for a moment. Pulling a pack of cigarettes from his pants pocket, he took one out and lit it. Then puffed the first smoke toward the sky.

"I gave Mr. Yumi my real name. And, I don't think he gave you all the information he knows."

"But he told you?"

"Maybe I ask better questions," she said, her eyes on Adams.

The detective flicked his cigarette and headed toward his own car.

Nicolo asked, "Like what?"

Juliet swung her legs into the car and shut the door. "Mr. Yumi speaks Korean."

"So?"

"So do the cooks at the Chinese restaurant."

"Okay…"

"Mr. Yumi knows what they're saying from the alley when he throws his trash out."

"Did he hear something I should know about?"

"He says he didn't."

"Juliet," he began with a voice impatient. "What would be helpful is to know where Paris is. Have you been in contact with him?"

"Yes," she admitted, glancing left and right, hoping to catch sight of said Paris. "But I don't know where he is right now."

"We'll trace your phone."

"I'm aware of that. Good thing I got a burner." And, she had. It was in her purse.

It sounded as though Nicolo dropped something

on the other end of the line. "What do you know about burner phones?"

"Abram told me…"

"Fontana?"

"Right. Abram also introduced me to the food at Panda Express. I've learned a lot from him."

"Does your grandmother know that you eat there? Never mind!" He sounded angrier with himself than at Juliet. "When was the last time you saw Nobleman?"

"No further questions," she told him and tapped the screen to end the phone call.

Tossing the phone on the seat, Juliet started the car, pulled it into the alley, and parked near the trees.

Had Noah waited back here for Jana to go to the bathroom? How would he know if she did? There was no view of the inside of the restaurant from the alley. No, if he killed Jana, he'd have to be able to watch her.

She cracked the passenger side window and listened.

She heard distant voices.

Out of the car, she slipped across the dirt alley and made for the trash dumpster.

The odor of fish eyes and wok grease came at her with aggressive energy.

Juliet swallowed down a gag reflex.

There was a window that sat high on the kitchen wall. It was the jalousie type, for ventilation. It was so easy to hear the cooks inside the kitchen.

Now, Juliet had visited China and Korea with her father years ago, but all she remembered right then was the word for wine: *Putaojiu*.

Wait, *Nong Kafei* meant espresso.

No one inside the kitchen spoke those words at the

moment, which meant Juliet was going to need to get by with what little Chinese she'd learned at the Panda Express.

She leaned past the trash dumpster. There was a door there. That's how the killer got inside, Juliet was sure of it. She crept forward, pulled on the knob, peeked inside. To the left was the kitchen. Straight ahead were the customer booths and tables. The ladies' room had to be on the right…

"*Mueos-eul chajgo issseubnikka?*" a man's voice said from behind her. "What are you doing here?"

Even before she turned around, Juliet knew the guy was big. What she'd heard was the sort of voice that came out of Sumo wrestlers.

She plastered a smile on her face and spun around.

Firstly, the guy wasn't that big. He couldn't have outweighed Juliet by twenty pounds, and secondly, it didn't matter how much the guy weighed because he carried a meat cleaver.

Which, you know, OMG.

"Italiano?" she asked, her voice wavering.

The fellow was very pretty, for a man, with his side-swept black hair, and delicate features. And those eyes, they were as wary as Juliet's—until they landed on the gold cross around her neck. He waved the cleaver in a small motion.

She swallowed the ball sized lump in her throat and touched her necklace. Thinking to distract him, she asked, "*Nong kafei?*"

His brows came together, and the sides of his eyes crinkled.

"*Putaojiu?*" Juliet tried again. "Kung Pao chicken?"

He said, in quite good English, "You want information about girl who died?" Sure, he was dropping his definite articles, but Juliet understood him.

She let out a hot breath. "God, yes."

"You pay for information?"

Cautious, she leaned her left side toward him. "How much?"

"Five hundred dollars."

"I don't carry that sort of cash."

"We have ATM inside," he said conversationally and pointed the meat cleaver over her head.

"What sort of information are we talking about?"

"I tell you when you pay me."

Okay, this is totally fine and not at all alarming.

Stepping aside, she let him enter the restaurant ahead of her. "Wait, I have to get my purse." She returned to the Fiat and grabbed her wallet out of her purse, and then followed the man inside. "What is your name?"

"Sang Ook."

Juliet followed Sang Ook–if that really was his name–beyond the kitchen and into the dimly lit dining room. There was a good-sized lunch crowd in the booths already, and it was only eleven o'clock.

Good, I like this. Plenty of witnesses…

Sang pointed to the corner and then waited by a small bar that stretched along the wall.

The restaurant carried the red theme inside. Red plastic covered the seats, and red tile made up the flooring. Even the neon ATM light was blinking red.

Once she had the money in her hand, she turned back around.

Sang motioned for her to join him behind the salad bar. He held out his slender fingers.

Juliet kept the cash close to her chest. "Tell me what

you saw before I give this to you."

He wagged his head back and forth. Was he deciding whether or not to tell her–or introduce her to the sharp end of the cleaver? "Old green car."

"I already know about the car. Did you see the person inside of it?"

His eyes drifted off for a moment. "Blonde hair."

"A woman?"

Sang shrugged one shoulder.

"Was the person large or small?"

"Person was in car."

Juliet waved the money at him. "You need to give me more than that, or this is going right back into the machine as a deposit."

"Person smoked. Flicked ash out opening in window." He held out one hand, near his head. "They have big hair."

"A wig?" Juliet prompted.

"Maybe."

She handed him the cash. "Did you tell the police what you've told me?"

He smiled, his teeth perfect and white. "It's none of my business until someone pulls money from the machine."

She let out a small gasp. Mr. Ook's lack of compassion and introspection was so disappointing. "You don't care that the person in the green car probably murdered someone?"

He gave her a slight bow. "Got to go cook now." He stuffed the cash into his apron pocket and turned away from her.

* * *

Paris had disappeared. Juliet drove around the building twice in an attempt to find him. A half hour later, she traveled back to the Novaks alone, got through the gate again and across the bridge.

Cyril had given Juliet a key to the house. Not a traditional metal key, but a visitor badge of sorts, because the Blonde Palace was straight up wired. The badge not only allowed Juliet access to the house, but it also controlled the temperature and music in her bedroom and lit the electric fireplace in her bathroom.

How will Paris get back inside?

He should've stayed close to the restaurant or to the car … why hadn't he jumped into the Fiat when Juliet jaunted off with shifty Sang Ook?

Detective Adams might have remained in the area, though. Maybe Paris simply walked away from the scene?

Opening the front door, Juliet was greeted by shiny marble floors and original pieces of art by Picasso and Kandinsky and Gauguin. Juliet had never been a fan of Kandinsky. Call her a snob, but the art didn't belong on the wall with Gauguin. And, Pablo, well … he had a funny way of looking at the world, didn't he? Where was Claude Monet in this mix? He was a guy who knew where to paint facial features.

Elevated voices interrupted Juliet's art study, and she turned toward the stairway. No one was there, so she moved around the bend in the wall.

A large doorframe stood sentry to a luxurious sitting room featuring an intricately carved fireplace, a chandelier, and three sets of arched wrought iron covered windows.

And there was Saskia and Juliet's mother near the windows; Italia stood next to an overstuffed chaise lounge.

On the chaise was Saskia, in a swoon position and dressed in silk pajamas that matched the furniture. Cream-colored puffballs accented her sandals. Saskia was Ava Gabor on a cellphone, speaking Czech to someone. Her eyes were terribly swollen.

Talk about a Picasso painting.

Juliet stepped farther into the room. "What's going on?"

Italia turned away from Saskia and crossed the room to stand in front of Juliet. She'd dressed in a silky pantsuit too. There was something different about her today, what was it, what was it…?

"We're having a bit of an emergency," she whispered.

Saskia spoke heatedly into the phone, and her voice broke. Was she crying? "Is she finally grieving Jana?"

"Of course she's grieving, Juliet. Don't talk like your father."

Peering over Italia's shoulder, she took a good look at Saskia. Bulging red flesh had replaced the woman's natural eyelids. "Whoa," she said under her breath. "Someone call Father John …"

"Hush," Italia said. "She's had a bad reaction to a Botox injection. She's talking to the doctor now."

Juliet winced. "It looks painful."

Saskia pulled the phone away from her ear, squinted at the screen, and pushed the end call button. "It is painful," she said, her voice taking on notes of a buzzing wasp. "The doctor is on his way back to the house."

Well, there was nothing wrong with her ears, was there?

Juliet bypassed her mother and stood next to the chaise. She'd never noticed before how much Saskia teased her blonde hair. It was perfectly coifed in the front and then puffed out behind her head like a jumbo marshmallow.

"Is that you, Juliet?" she asked, reaching out.

"Yes."

"It's so difficult to see…"

"I can imagine."

A shadow crossed in front of the window, and Saskia turned that direction. "Who's out there, Juliet? Is it the doctor already?"

Juliet glanced out the window and saw men loping along toward the pool. There were three of them dressed in long bathing pants and no shirts. She said, "It's Hugo and his friends."

"Hugo's gang," Saskia said, leaning back on the chaise again and squinting at Juliet. "Hugo's popular, you know? He has so many friends."

"I like him very much too. He's fun."

"Fun?" Saskia said and laughed as though that was quite a joke. She waved at the window. "Tell me, is that Gerald boy out there too?"

Juliet leaned farther toward the window.

Hugo had jumped into the pool and floated backward away from Gerald.

Gerald sat on the edge of the pool, in yellow swim trunks.

How do they stand the cold?

"Yes, Gerald is there, and Noah York."

"Yes, yes," Saskia murmured. "They all want to go on adventures together. Can you imagine, they want to go to Australia and walkabout, whatever that is."

"Haven't you seen *Crocodile Dundee*?" Juliet asked.

Saskia practically came off the lounger. "Crocodiles? What do you mean?"

"Crocodiles …" Juliet said. "The Australian croc is generally considered the most dangerous in the world." She glanced at her mother for confirmation. "They have the worst predators there: snakes, dingoes, great white sharks…"

"Juliet," her mother interrupted.

"What?"

But then she saw what: Saskia was hyperventilating and clutching the silk top against her chest. "Hugo will not be going to Australia. I thought they wanted to visit Sydney and see the opera house."

Juliet wasn't sure, but this seemed a disproportionate response out of Saskia.

Italia stepped forward and took Juliet's arm. "Why don't you join Hugo and his friends? Take a dip in the pool."

"Because it's twenty-seven degrees outside."

"It's heated," Saskia said, pulling herself together.

"I mean the air."

"So do I," the woman told her. "The heating system reaches fifty yards outside the house."

Oh!

That's why her balcony had felt so warm last night…

Italia draped her arm into Juliet's. "Juliet is just a fish in the water."

Saskia nodded. "I do smell fish right now. Isn't that funny? Just the suggestion of it."

Italia lifted her nose, and then stared at Juliet.

Juliet backed away, knowing it was she who reeked of Jinlin's wok grease. "I'll go change," she told her mother and turned toward the door quickly–and almost ran into *another* birdcage. There were two birds inside this one, beautifully bright green, orange, and red ones. The birds sat quite close on the perch together. "You have so many birds now," Juliet said, turning back around. "I don't remember seeing them when I was here in February."

"Oh, they're Hugo's new obsession," Saskia said. "Noah's influence again. Noah's been to Madagascar and Southern Africa. He talks about the species of birds there."

"I think they're beautiful," Italia said. "Juliet loves birds, don't you, dear?"

She bit her lip, thinking about that. Did she love birds? "They're nice enough, I suppose. Are the chickens Hugo's pets, too?"

"Oh no," Saskia said, leaning again on the back of the tufted chair. "Those were a gift from Cyril to his sister, Xenia. He gave them to her, and I don't know what she thinks of them. Cyril is often mad. He's going through a bird phase himself."

And a cigarette phase, too, Juliet thought, leaving the room and rounding the wall to the stairs. She was on the second floor landing when Mali came across the bridge.

At first, Juliet didn't recognize the girl because she wore a wig—a costly one by the looks of it. The hair was brunette and cut in a straight bob. Mali's makeup: flawless.

Teagan followed behind, as usual, wearing a white jumpsuit with Yeezy sneakers. What did the girl do to make money to afford Yeezys? Teagan didn't work, she couldn't; she was at Mali's side. All. The. Time.

Does Mali pay her?

If she did, what did she pay Teagan to do, hang out and hold a camera steady?

Juliet stood off to the side, to let the girls pass.

Mali's eyes landed on Juliet, and she held out her arms. "Here she is again," she announced to her social media audience. She turned and faced Teagan and the camera. "If you didn't see my last post, which I'm sure you did, this is one of our houseguests."

Juliet widened her eyes. Was she supposed to say something to the Instagram followers?

"Isn't she gorg?" Mali asked, without waiting for a response. She twirled her finger in the air.

Teagan evidently knew what the twirling finger meant, because she walked all the way around Juliet, pointing the camera at her.

Mali said, "Juliet is wearing Cavalli jeans and jacket, which are mine. The poor girl didn't have a stitch to wear when she arrived."

Juliet opened her mouth to protest.

Mali spoke over her. "In tomorrow's segment, we'll see if my stylist can do anything with that hair."

Juliet lifted her hand to her curly hair. Where were the brakes to this fashion show?

Mali turned to Teagan. "Why am I smelling fish?" Her pale eyes returned to Juliet. "Have you been to Jinlin's Dine-In?"

Juliet dropped her hand to her side. "Have you?"

"Draw if you be men."

Chapter 10

We haven't been in ages," Teagan said, and then flashed Mali a glance. "Unless you went without me."

Mali shook her head, but stopped mid-shake, as though she'd thought of something. Without a word, she moved down the steps toward the first floor.

Teagan watched her go. "I can't believe she went without me."

"I can't believe she knew I was just there."

"You smell like wok grease."

Juliet palmed her curly hair again and then sniffed her hand. *Time for a rinse.*

Teagan remained on the landing. "What exactly are you up to?"

Juliet glanced to the left and then back at Teagan. "What do you mean?"

"I saw you sneaking into the house last night."

Suddenly Juliet couldn't breathe. Had Teagan seen Paris sneaking into the house too?

Of course she didn't. She would've called security.

Unless she thought Paris was security, or staff.

"Oh, you should see your face," Teagan said, her eyes bright with satisfaction.

Juliet shook her head. "What do you think I was doing? I'd only gone for a walk."

"I *think* you were looking for Noah."

"What if I was?"

Teagan lifted her chin. "Stay away from him." Shoving past Juliet, she descended the stairs.

* * *

Juliet stood in the shower for thirty minutes, rinsing out her hair, and thinking about what Teagan had said. Sure, Noah was a good looking guy, but what was all the fuss?

He'd been engaged to Jana. Didn't Teagan care about that?

Wait … maybe Teagan did care about that, so much so that she killed Jana over it.

See, being jealous of someone is wrong. And killing someone, that is also wrong.

Face to the ceiling, Juliet's mind drifted off to the Yumi Flower Shop.

Yumi had seen Bexley in the alley on the day of the murder. That made sense. Bexley had been stalking Jana again—or Noah, who was in the old green car.

Or, Teagan had been in the green car.

Most importantly: who drives a green car?

Juliet shut off the water and took a super fluffy towel from the rack outside the stall. She rubbed her face and worked on her hair.

Suddenly, Juliet thought of the vintage autos in the showroom downstairs.

Hey!

Standing straighter, she wrapped the towel around her shoulders. Had Yumi and Sang described a vintage car?

* * *

Juliet slipped into another pair of jeans, pulled her wet hair into a bun, and exited her room. Carefully. She poked her head around the corner of the wall.

Was there truly a need to sneak?

Why yes, yes there was, because Juliet didn't know where Ms. Stalkerpants Teagan was at the moment. Sure, the girl had gone downstairs, but that was forty-five minutes ago. Was she watching the hallway from a crack in Mali's bedroom door right now?

Juliet straightened her posture and walked down the hallway naturally.

Just heading downstairs like an average person … no intention of breaking into the vintage car garage.

She'd judged that the glassed-in garage was on the same side of the house as her bedroom. Juliet needed only to go to the ground floor.

The lower level hallway was a half a football field in length. Passages jutted left and right off the main corridor. One led to the spa wing, and another opened into a movie theater.

Around the last curve was the glass door to the vintage cars. Or, as that DIY show called it: the Garage Mahal.

Juliet pushed on the door.

It opened easily.

What was wrong with Cyril Novak that he kept his garage door wide open? Didn't he know what sort of people were in his house?

Me for one.

Sunshine coming in through the three glass walls lit the vintage collection. Fenders sparkled in the sun's rays. It was like a beach for cars, but there was no suntan lotion smell, only a hint of chrome polish and leather cleaner.

On each platform was a small sign stating the year and make of the vehicle. The first car on display was a 1910 Rolls-Royce Silver Ghost. In the streaming sunlight, it appeared more lavender than silver.

Juliet moved farther into the garage, beyond the '27 LaSalle, and a black 1915 Cadillac. She spun around, bending at the waist, and ducking here and there.

Toward the front … yes, toward the front, she saw green paint, and suddenly Juliet knew the sweet bracing satisfaction of being right.

A clicking noise interrupted her euphoria.

Instinctively, Juliet flattened herself against the wall. Was someone else in the garage, or was a car engine cooling off?

A car door slammed. "Dammit!"

Had it been a man or a woman's voice? It was so hard

to tell in an echoing garage.

Juliet ducked again, watching for movement between the platforms.

There!

Legs in brown trousers moved toward the door.

Juliet stepped sideways, creeping on the sides of her feet.

Could it be that the brown-trousered person had a legitimate reason to be in the garage? Perhaps it was a service employee, working on a *green* car–or maybe it was Cyril strolling among the beauties of his car garden.

Juliet lifted her voice, "Hello," and planned to create a story about interest in vintage cars for her father's sake.

The person stopped moving.

Juliet froze too, eyes widening and holding her breath.

So, maybe the brown-trousered person didn't have a legitimate reason to be in the garage.

Something hit the wall above Juliet's head.

She ducked and then shot a glance behind her.

A wrench had hit the wall and now spun like a top toward one of the platforms.

The person had gone *hood* on her!

A tiny spark of anger started in her belly. Juliet snatched the wrench and held it in front of her.

That's all right. We can go hood.

Footsteps pounded toward the hallway door.

Juliet jumped and ran too–straight into one of the platforms.

She fell forward, her knees catching the floor. Pain shot through her left leg. "This is excellent," she said, exhaling the agony, and inhaling the curing. When she got back to her room, she'd put a piece of gum on it, and it'd be fine.

Standing, she limped toward the door and hobbled into the hallway.

No one was there.

She hobbled forward anyway, around the curve, and holding the wrench up. She peered down the first hallway.

Had the wrench-thrower chose the dark movie theater to hide in?

Juliet started off again.

A door opened.

She spun around, wrench at the ready.

Cyril stepped out of what looked like a small bathroom. He smelled of smoke and tobacco. He hadn't looked up, was shutting the door, and then turned.

Slipping the wrench behind her back, she squeaked, "Hi."

Cyril swayed backward, and both of his hands came out and grabbed the doorjamb to stop from falling.

"Sorry," she told him, reaching for him, and dropping the wrench at the same time.

He steadied himself. "Good God, what are you shouting about?"

"Um," she started, and bent for the wrench. "You surprised me."

"I surprised you?" His blonde shag rug of a toupee tipped slightly to the left. Cyril was dressed much more formally than, well, Juliet at least. He wore black pants and a coat and a white shirt. "Is that a wrench?"

"Yes, it is," she told him, hoping that was all the information he needed. "Did you see or hear anyone run past here?"

"Were you chasing them with a household tool?" He adjusted the knot of his silk tie.

"Oh, no, no." She bit her lip and looked up and down the hallway. Whoever ran out of the garage was on the other side of the house by now. To get off the *wrench subject*, Juliet said, "I saw you smoking yesterday."

That's right, put him on the defense.

Cyril's eyes widened. "Where did you see me?"

"You used my bathroom. Third-floor, guest bedroom."

"Oh," he said, sounding disappointed. "I guess the jig is up."

She lifted a shoulder. "Why not just tell everyone, and then you can smoke wherever you please?"

He smiled and started walking down the hall. "Have you met my wife?"

Juliet moved with him. "Ever thought about quitting?"

"The marriage? Why, yes, I have."

She let out a laugh, a weak one. Her knee was on fire. "The cigarettes."

"Oh," he said, his head bobbing, and then, "No."

"But you're the only one who smokes."

"Saskia used to light up now and then. She expected me to quit when she did." He turned down another corridor.

Juliet followed. "Does Noah smoke?"

Cyril stopped and turned. "Well, I don't know. I'm not in the habit of watching Mr. York." He held up his index finger. "He's a vigorous person. Maybe he was the one running in the hallway."

"Maybe," Juliet agreed. "Whoever it was came out of your snazzy garage." She held up the wrench again. "As did this."

"Is that so?"

"Yes, it is. My father restores Italian cars."

Cyril had his hand on the doorknob. "I admire your

father. He's successful at many things." He turned the knob. "I don't restore the cars that I buy. I'm more of a collector."

"Are all of the vintage cars yours?"

"Yes." He still hadn't straightened his toupee. Maybe he didn't want to touch it in front of Juliet. Perhaps he thought she'd been fooled into thinking it was his real hair. "There are other garages on the property, as I'm sure you're aware, but this one is temperature controlled for the body paint and leatherwork on the cars."

Juliet pursed her lips and then asked, "Anyone ever take a spin in them?"

"Around the estate, yes. Not in the city."

She nodded nonchalantly. "Are the keys laying out somewhere?"

His dark brows climbed his forehead. "Would you like to take one out for a spin? You're most welcome to do so."

Juliet shook her head. "Maybe later. I'm just … well, I'm curious. Has anyone borrowed one of your cars without asking?"

His mouth pulled down at the corners. "What are you getting at?"

"There have been sightings of your green car in the city recently."

"Really?" he asked, his voice climbing. His eyes narrowed, and he leaned an inch closer. "That's not possible. No one's borrowed a car."

"How do you know?"

He shook his head. "They'd have to ask for the key. All the keys are in a locked box."

"Someone could've picked the lock," Juliet said. "Have you checked recently?"

He pushed open the door, and lights came on automatically. It was an office area with high ceilings and arched doorways. A cherry wood desk sat on one side of the room, guest chairs were in front, and beneath the furniture was an exquisite Persian rug in light and dark blues. An accent wall of terracotta brought out the highlights of the wood and bookcases and the hardwood flooring.

Cyril stepped behind the desk and opened a drawer. Pulling out a case, he set it in front of him, took a set of keys from his pocket, and opened the case. "As you can see, the lock is secure." He slipped one of the compartments forward and checked the inventory of car keys. "Nothing is missing." He glanced her direction, eyebrows up. "You see?"

Juliet glanced around the room, considering the art and then the ceilings and the corners of the walls. "You have surveillance in the house?"

Cyril came around the desk and moved toward the closet. He opened the door wide.

Juliet joined him.

Inside the closet were surveillance equipment and several monitors. Cyril hit one of the keys on the pad and then leaned closer to the screen. "That's odd. It's been turned off." He hit another button and then checked one of the cords.

"Someone turned it off?"

"Or it turned off by itself. Computers have glitches once in a while."

The screens brightened all at the same time. And then the pictures came up, one of the gate at the front of the property, another at the front, side, and back doors. Several of the monitors showed different areas inside the house, mostly the hallways.

"Do you know how long the system has been off?"

Cyril leaned closer to the screen, gazing at the bottom right of it. "Good Lord. It's been off for three weeks. How strange."

"Who else has access to the system?"

He shook his head. "No one. I'm the only one who has the password." Stepping away, he shut the door. "All's well now. The system is on," he waved toward his desk, "and the keys are in order."

"Right," Juliet agreed. "All is well." She turned toward the hallway door.

Cyril called to her. "Remember, mum's the word about cigarettes."

She turned around at the doorway with her hand on the knob. "Your secret is safe with me." And then, she shut the door.

Juliet slipped inside the Garage Mahal again and waited for the glass door to close behind her.

Everything was quiet.

Would Brown Trousers come back?

Juliet moved quickly and quietly toward the glass windows—and there it was, a green 1961 Chevrolet Corvair.

Was this the car that Yumi and Sang described as an old green car?

Well, if it wasn't, then why had Brown Trousers thrown a wrench at her head?

There's definitely something going on here.

Juliet touched the hood of the Corvair.

It was cold.

Glancing left and right, she made for the driver's side door and pulled it open.

Nothing about the interior stood out to her–other than how sparse looking it was compared to the gadgets on the Fiat dash. The seat was a bench type; the steering wheel was the size of a hula hoop.

Juliet closed the door gently and cupped her face to see into the back seat through the window.

Again, nothing stood out. But then, Juliet wasn't sure what she was looking for anyway. She turned toward the garage windows and looked out each in turn. How did a person drive out of the garage anyway?

At the top of the windows was a mechanical wheel. It seemed all sides of the glass moved with the mechanism. Just beyond the window was a ramp that led to a small driveway that disappeared into the woods.

There were tire marks in the lawn, but Juliet had no idea how long they'd been there. She turned toward the car, to check the tires on the Chevrolet…

Something else caught her attention.

There was a good view of the south side of the house through the last window, including the house and the chimney. It wasn't the chimney that was so remarkable, but the color of the smoke that came out of it. It was green.

Hmm.

She dismissed the phenomenon and gazed at the tires on the Corvair.

They were clean, as though the car hadn't been driven for a long time. But, there on the platform rug was a bit of dry white dirt. It wasn't much. It only meant that the killer had missed a spot.

"Let's talk, it is not day."

Chapter 11

Back in her room, Juliet sat on the balcony and rubbed her sore knee.

Who'd thrown a wrench at her?

Noah had been poolside an hour ago; Gerald too. That left plenty of time to dry off and change into brown pants.

What about Teagan? The last Juliet saw the girl she'd been wearing white. Then again, she'd had time to change clothes and head to the garage.

She leaned back in the chair and stared up at the dark sky. There were few stars to see since the clouds draped in front of them like gauzy spider webs.

There'd been nothing in the car. Nothing Juliet had been hoping to find, anyway, like balloon strings or a helium tank. She was positive, however, that she'd found the right car. The killer had followed Jana in the Corvair–maybe only intending to speak privately to her away from the house. Whoever it was sat in the Corvair for a time, smoking and flicking ashes, and staring at balloon ribbons … finally, they got out of the car, opened the back door to the restaurant, and waited near the restroom for Jana.

Juliet chewed the cuticle on her left thumb. Then what happened? The killer asked to speak to Jana. Jana obviously knew the person and stepped outside with them.

Sitting straighter, Juliet leaned forward to rethink.

If Jana and the killer argued, someone would've heard it. Someone would've seen something.

But they didn't, so…

There was no argument. The killer didn't go to the restaurant to talk to Jana. He or she had thought it all out beforehand. The killer had been to the restaurant before, knew where the bathroom was, waited quietly, asked Jana outside, and choked her before she could cry out.

What about the balloon ties?

It was an added touch, just to throw everybody off, to make the police think the murder wasn't premeditated … that it was a robbery turned deadly with a kiss balloon.

Thus with a kiss, she died.

Absolutely, the killer was someone in the Novak house. Whether it was one of the Novaks, or one of their friends—Teagan, Gerald, or Noah—it was someone who knew how to turn off the security cameras.

Juliet supposed it wasn't too tricky to turn them off, especially if you knew about cameras or computers. And the keys to the cars were conveniently in the same room as the security computer.

But why take a vintage car? Surely a vintage model was more noticeable than some other vehicle.

Was the killer attempting to frame Cyril?

Juliet sat straighter. That was certainly a possibility.

Or it was Cyril himself who was the murderer? He'd come out of the bathroom at the right moment, stinking of smoke. Had he time to light a cigarette and change his pants?

Juliet shook her head. No, no way.

Maybe.

She sat back again and thought it all through once more.

Night fell, and all the lights in the pool came on. One of the house employees lit the fire pit, even though there was no one around to enjoy it at the moment.

I want Limoncello.

The lemon liqueur always helped Juliet think more clearly, especially out on a balcony while listening to crickets and frogs serenading her. Perhaps she should drive back to the vineyard and grab a bottle to keep with her in the bedroom. It was a bit of a drive, forty or forty-five minutes each way.

Juliet pushed to her feet. Finding her boots near the bed, she stepped into them. From where she stood, she had a view of the courtyard and lawns on the western side of the house. Uplighting hit the ferns and landscape plantings … and an escaped chicken.

It was still strange to Juliet, that billionaires kept chickens–be they beautiful chickens with silky feathers. They were the sort of bird that, if eaten, would only be used in the finest recipes, Poulet de Provencal or Coq au Vin.

Suddenly, the chicken fluttered away, as though it had been startled by something, and it disappeared into the ferns.

Juliet leaned forward.

Someone walked near the tree line. Was the person on the way to Noah's cottage?

No, they headed in the opposite direction, toward one of the doors of the main house.

Paris?

Juliet hurried out of her room, and moved cautiously past Mali's bedroom door, just in case Teagan thought to spy on her again.

The door was completely shut.

Juliet made for the stairs and hobbled down as fast as she could with her painful knee. No one else seemed to be around. Everything was very quiet … Juliet kept her eyes on the set of French doors at the end of the great room.

A shadow moved to the left.

Juliet moved to the left too and then pushed open the swinging kitchen doors and waited.

There was recessed lighting in the ceiling and a massive island in the center of the room. Black granite counters glistened and so did the glazed cabinets.

At last, the shadow moved upward on the glass part of the door.

Juliet reached for the doorknob to let the person inside. But, the door opened on it's own when someone else flung it open.

"AIIAIIGH!"

Juliet's heart bolted into her throat.

Hugo continued screaming and slapped at Juliet with

both his hands. He was a cat batting a toy mouse, but never actually hitting her.

"Stop it," she told him, air-swatting him in return. "Stop it, you maniac."

Hugo paused with his paws in the air. His small mouth opened. "Juliet?"

"Yes!"

"Oh god, I think I peed a little."

She tried not to laugh. "I was just opening the door for you." Turning, she took a seat at the kitchen island. She needed to catch her breath and massage her knee after coming down two flights of stairs that were easily fifty steps each … and now this, this cat game.

Hugo stepped inside and pulled the door shut behind him. "Why do you think you need to open the door for me?"

"I don't know. What's with the fifty questions?" There was an opened bottle of wine on the counter, and she slid it toward her. "I just came down to get a drink." There was no glass within reach, so she took a swig, meaning to claim the entire bottle and keep it in her room.

A little too late, Hugo said, "I wouldn't do that…"

Yes, it was much too late. The wine hit Juliet's tongue and visions of socks soaking in a dirty sink–in a third world country somewhere–came to her mind.

Off the chair, she rushed toward the sink and spat the wine out of her mouth. "Ugh! What is this?" She held up the bottle and stared at the label.

"My father's first attempt at apple wine."

She ran water in the sink and rinsed her mouth. "*Dios Mio*, it tastes worse than Boone's Farm, and, and … murder."

Hugo's grin widened. "Not worth opening the door for me, was it?"

She set the bottle aside and found a paper towel to wipe her lips. "You scared me too, you know. What were you doing sneaking in from the garden?"

"I wasn't." He stood straighter. "There was no sneaking."

He reeked of lies.

Juliet approached him, eyes narrowed. "You're guilty of something."

"I'm a free man. Stop asking me questions."

She stepped closer, very near him, and took a long breath through her nose. "You smell like …" Juliet raised her eyes and placed the odors. "Newports, Heineken, and Slim Jims."

He leaned away from her. "I don't smoke."

"Well, whoever you were with was smoking."

Hugo grinned. "Smoking hot!"

She dropped her eyes to his overcoat and the plaid shirt underneath. "What's in your pocket? Are those your under…?"

"None of your business." He covered his pocket with his hand.

She shrugged and backed off. "It is, if you expect me to accept your marriage proposal."

Hugo gasped. "You've reconsidered?"

"No, and I don't care what's in your pocket either."

Stepping around her, he pulled out whatever was in his pocket, walked to an open door across the kitchen, and threw whatever it was into the other room.

"Is that your bedroom?"

"I had to get away from the constant vlogging on the other side of the house. There's no privacy up there." He opened the refrigerator and gazed inside. "And, Teagan, she won't leave me alone."

"She likes you?" And here, Juliet had thought Teagan rather liked Noah York.

Hugo faced her, hand on the fridge door. "I am attractive."

"Yes, you are," Juliet agreed, nodding. "But does Teagan know you're, you know …?"

"She knows I'm gay. She just wants to be Mali's sister-in-law."

"But that's what you want. That's why you want to marry me, to get your parents off your back."

"No," he said, flinging out his hands. "I want to come live with you, Juliet. Teagan will be in this house forever."

"Oh, I see." Her eyes drifted toward his bedroom door. Was it really a bedroom? She stepped that way and glanced into the room.

It wasn't a bedroom, but a sitting room, with chairs facing a fireplace. Hugo's underwear lay right in the middle of the floor.

Please brain, forget you ever saw his tighty whities.

Her brain brought up something else. Juliet turned toward Hugo. "Were you throwing something into the fireplace today?" Thinking back, she remembered the placement of the chimney, that it would be right about at this spot in the house. "Something green, perhaps."

Hugo didn't answer.

The outside door had opened again. This time Xenia stood in the doorway. "What are you two doing?" Her gaze went from Hugo to Juliet, and to the door behind Juliet. "Sorry," she said, holding up her hand. "None of my business."

Am I the only one who knows that Hugo is gay?

Hugo shoved the refrigerator door shut. "Where are you coming from, Auntie?"

Xenia stepped toward the island and placed something in one of the baskets in the center of the counter. Then she shrugged out of her coat. "I was checking on the chickens." She nodded to the basket. "My first egg."

"Wow," Hugo said, glancing at Juliet and rolling his eyes. "I don't know what to say. Congratulations, I guess."

"Yes, congratulations. Of course, congratulations," Xenia said. Her hair flopped into her eyes, like one of the chickens outside. "I'll eat it for breakfast."

"Is it okay to eat?" Hugo asked her, eyeing the egg.

"Of course."

"It's blue, though."

"It's perfectly normal," Xenia told him, throwing her coat over her arm. "Now, if you'll excuse me," she said, more to Juliet than to Hugo. She skirted around her and headed toward the front room and, presumably, the stairs.

"So, what's her story?" Juliet asked, coming back to the island. Had Xenia really been outside on the search for chicken eggs when most people collected them in the morning? Not that Juliet was an expert at farming, but she had read *Little House on the Prairie* when she was a kid.

Hugo had leaned on the kitchen counter with the support of his elbow. He held the egg between his fingers. "Auntie is fantafreakintabulous. She should've been my mother."

Juliet sat again on the counter chair and watched Hugo turn the egg over. "Really? Why?"

"Because she jumps out of airplanes and hikes canyons." He set the egg on the counter and cupped his broad chin in the palm of his hand. "I want to be like that, but Sergeant Mother thinks I might break a nail if I get vigorous." He studied the index finger on his free hand.

Guilt washed over her as Juliet remembered how Saskia responded after the mention of crocodiles and great white sharks. "She's protective. Your mother loves you."

"Oh, is that what it is, love?" He let his hand drop on the counter. "I'd rather not be loved so much. If Xenia were my mother, we'd be off to Australia tomorrow. She's offered to come with us, but the sergeant threw a cow at us for even talking about it."

Juliet sat back in the seat. "Do your mom and Xenia get along most of the time?"

"I think they avoid each other," Hugo said, his shoulders sagging forward. "Xenia is my father's sister, not my mother's."

"Why does she live here?"

"It's home base, I suppose. She's gone nine months of the year, cycling, rowing, and having huge, life-changing, life-enhancing adventures."

"You told me she met Noah on an adventure."

"Did I?" he asked, turning his eyes her way. "I think she did, but Noah isn't even in her league, adventure-wise. I think she had to save him before he fell into a volcano."

"She brought him home with her, you said."

"I think he followed her here, to be honest." He tapped the bluish egg with one finger, causing it to spin. "I'm not sure she likes him very much. I mean, I think she did at first, but ever since Jana died, she complains about him, and wants him out of the house."

"Does she think Noah killed Jana?"

Hugo's head snapped around. His features contorted into what—fear, or rage? "What are you talking about?"

He pushed off the counter and shoved the egg by accident.

Juliet jumped forward in her chair, reaching for it and then watching it roll off the edge.

Hugo turned around just as the egg fell. He tried to catch it, but it was too late.

A sickening splat sounded on the stone flooring.

Hugo's eyes widened. "Oh my god, Juliet. Help!"

Her mouth was open long before the word, "How?" came out.

"I don't know. Can we put it back together?"

"With what, Superglue?" Off the chair, she rounded the island.

"Yes?" He grabbed a paper towel from the sink area. Then he just stood there, looking down at the dead yolk.

"It's gone, Hugo."

His eyes found hers. "Run."

"What?" she asked, her eyes just as round as his.

"Run!" Dropping the towel, he flew toward the other door in the kitchen. He went around the corner; his sneakers squeaked as he gained traction.

Juliet stood still for a moment, watching him. Then she ran away too.

* * *

Juliet dreamed of snakes. She didn't see them but heard their hissing. The sound came closer, closer …

She jolted awake and sat up in the bed, which made her stomach nauseous.

The snakes still hissed. Then they were on the bed, making the mattress bounce with their weight.

Juliet shook her head.

Mali and Teagan sat on the bed in front of her.

Pulling the covers to her midsection, she said, "Hi?"

"It's makeover morning," Mali squealed and glanced at the camera.

Teagan moved the camera closer.

"Oh, right …"

"First, we dress you, and then we meet the hairdresser in the studio." Mali turned toward Teagan. "I need to stand up."

The girl shifted backward on the bed.

"Come on," Mali said. "Don't be camera shy, Juliet. My fans have seen much more skin than what you're showing right now."

Juliet shoved at the bedcovers and put her feet on the floor. Darn right her fans had seen more skin on Mali than they ever would on Juliet Da Vinci.

The fireplace still had a low flame, and the room felt toasty, too. One of the girls smelled like fresh roses. Juliet climbed out of bed and followed the girls to the walk-in closet.

Teagan reached for the black catsuit hanging on the rack.

"Perfect," Mali said and handed it to Juliet. "Put this on. No bra is necessary. There are cups inside the bodice."

"This really isn't my style," Juliet said, draping the suit over one arm.

"Right." Mali leaned nearer. She wore her long white and gold tresses down this morning. Already she'd expertly applied her eye shadows—browns and creams—and wore traceless foundation. Her lips, oxblood red. "That's why we're doing the makeover, Juliet. To widen your choices in hair and makeup and clothing." She gazed at the camera.

"It's so easy to find a style and stay with it too long, people. The world is full of color and choices, some good, some bad, but change up your world once in a while. You'll feel better about yourself." She bent, selected the long boots on the floor, and took them into the bedroom.

Posture slumped, Juliet turned toward the bathroom.

"Wait, you'll need these," Mali told her and tossed a pair of Insta-Booty panties in the air.

Juliet caught them and held them up. "Oh, no."

"Come on, Juliet," Mali pleaded. "This is for our followers."

"I've got enough butt."

Both Teagan and Mali shook their heads, and Mali pointed toward the bathroom.

I really don't like either one of them now.

Fitting the Insta-Bootie onto her bottom Juliet turned around in the full-length mirror. Who was she supposed to be, J-Lo? Oh, if Tribly could see her now.

Tribly would stick a fork in her butt and try to deflate it.

Juliet pulled on the catsuit and tied up her hair with a long scarf. Returning to the bedroom, Juliet found the camera on her again.

"Look at that ass," Teagan said with appreciation. She was dressed in a silver catsuit herself, but with strappy sandals. Hers was more of a tank top affair. There was a patch on her arm that Juliet had never noticed.

"Is that a nicotine patch, Teagan?" she asked, sitting on the chaise and slipping her leg into the first thigh-high boot. "I didn't know you smoked."

"I don't," she said, still filming. "I just like the buzz it gives me."

Juliet slipped her foot into the other boot. "Have you heard of espresso?" She got to her feet, wobbling a little in the six inch heels. "Speaking of, I'd like to grab a coffee before heading to the studio."

"It's downstairs," Teagan told her, switching off the camera.

Yes, Juliet remembered the watered-down stuff from yesterday. She really needed to return home for some supplies: Limoncello, espresso, and any other o's she might require.

On the stairs, voices rose up from the kitchen area. By the time they were on the second landing, Juliet understood the words: "I set my egg right here. Did you cook it?"

Uh oh.

Another voice, a man's and just as loud, returned fire. "There was no egg on the counter. I did clean one up that had splattered on the floor."

Juliet hesitated on the last step. Would Xenia ask her about the egg? After all, Juliet was one of the last to see the little thing.

I'll crack…

She said, "Never mind the coffee. Let's just do my hair."

On the first floor, they cut beneath the opposite stairway and through a back hallway. Juliet saw another garage through a glass door, but with ordinary cars, not vintage models. And, the vehicles were parked in the standard method and not up on pedestals. This was something she could get behind, people acting normally, and parking horizontally in the spaces provided.

Mali led the way through the final doorway.

The smell of warm blow-dried hair hit Juliet first, and

then notes of shampoo and hair product above that. Two black leather styling chairs faced white framed mirrors fitted with bulb lights all the way around them. Canned lights overhead beamed down on the work areas. A fireplace was lit on the south side of the room.

Teagan lifted the camera and pointed it at Mali.

Mali swept her hand toward a woman standing next to the styling chairs. "Juliet, this is Cammie. She's my favorite stylist."

Cammie was in her forties and was possibly Hawaiian. She wore a baggy golden knit sweater and tight jeans. There were black plastic gloves on her hand, as though she thought there might be a dye job in Juliet's future.

How wrong you are, Hawaii Girl.

Mali waved to one of the chairs. "Have a seat, Juliet." She eyed her friend. "Teagan, move in. Get both Juliet and me in the camera view." Mali leaned against the equipment counter jutting from the wall. "Tell us about your current beauty regime," she asked, nodding to Juliet.

Juliet let out a long breath. "Um, mani/pedi every three or four weeks."

Mali leaned back. "Seriously? Mine is weekly. I love to change my colors."

She took the camera from Teagan and moved toward the other side of the room where nail color bottles lined the wall behind a nail bar.

Teagan had lost interest and stood at a multi-paned window on the north side of the room. She stared across the lawn.

Juliet gazed out the window, too, toward Noah York's cottage.

And there was Noah, dressed in tight jeans and a

bomber jacket. He walked beside ruby-haired Gerald.

Teagan turned away from the window with a snarl firmly set on her upper lip.

Cammie came at Juliet with both her hands in the air. She'd spread her fingers out as though she meant to attack something.

"In bed asleep while they do dream things true."

Chapter 12

Stiff fingers mashed through Juliet's curls. Then the hands lifted the hair at Juliet's neck and caused her chin to hit her chest. She was left to stare at a wastebasket. Inside was a *Kerastase* color kit, a very high end product. Was that what kept the Palace Blonde?

And then, Mali was back, still recording. "What about facials, Juliet? How often?"

She spoke to her belly, "Every couple of months."

"If you're not going to take this seriously…"

"That's how often I have them," Juliet said.

Cammie had a death grip on her head and yanked backward.

"What about your hair?"

"Um, cut every six weeks, and I use Voss products."

"Brows?"

"Waxed every three weeks."

Mali turned the camera toward the mirror and filmed herself from that angle. "And that's how people get into a mess with their self-care programs," she told her audience. "Fortunately, for Juliet, all of that will change today." She turned the camera onto the stylist. "Please begin."

"First, we're going to wash her hair and add moisturizer. Lots of it," Cammie told the camera.

It wasn't as though her hair was in that bad of shape. "I do have a stylist," she told the woman.

Cammie's dark eyes remained on Juliet's hair. "Have they never suggested thinning some of it out?"

"I don't want it thinned."

Juliet caught Teagan mouthing *thin it* to Cammie.

It took forty-five minutes for Cammie to wash and condition Juliet's hair. By the time she sat in the stylist chair again, Mali had lost interest and had gone into the hallway for something.

Teagan followed her.

Cammie rubbed Juliet's hair with a towel for another five minutes and then tossed the cloth toward the hamper in the corner of the room. "I know who you are," she said.

Juliet peered at Cammie in the mirror. "You do?"

"Yes," she said, grabbing a brush from the counter. "I read the BuzzFeed article last year. You're Juliet of *Juliet and Dead Romeo*, right?"

"Right, that's me."

"It's amazing that you found the killer." Shaking her head in apparent disbelief, Cammie brushed again and brushed some more. Then she switched to a comb that looked suspiciously like a razor comb.

But Juliet wasn't so much concerned about that at the moment. It hit her that Cammie was a fan of mystery. Maybe she could answer some questions about what went on around this house when Jana died. "I'd like to find the killer this time, too."

Cammie caught her breath and leaned forward. "Is that what you're doing here?"

"Not officially, no. My mother is a friend of Saskia's." She adjusted the cape on her lap and spread it further onto her knees. "Where were you when they found out about Jana's murder?"

The woman smacked Juliet on top of the head with the comb.

Juliet jumped in surprise.

"I arrived at the same time the police did. I was supposed to do Jana's hair that day." She worked the back of Juliet's hair. "When the police ushered everyone into the front room, I stayed in the hallway and peeked around the doorway."

"You sound just like me," Juliet told her. "I would've done the same thing."

The canned light twinkled in Cammie's eyes.

"How'd everyone take it? They don't seem to be grieving too much."

"Right?" Cammie hit Juliet's head again with the comb, tossed it on the counter, and pulled long scissors from her pocket. "Mr. Novak took it the worst. He was the blood relation to Jana. But the rest of the family just sat there and listened. They're so cold like that. Self-absorbed, you know?"

"Who all was there? I mean, was Hugo's friend in the room too?"

"No," she said, shaking her very dark head. "To be fair, Hugo was shocked too, but you never know with him. He's such an actor."

"What about Teagan?"

Cammie glanced behind her to make sure the girl wasn't in earshot. She moved closer. "That girl. I really don't remember if she was there or not. I assume she was, since she's always got her nose so far up Mali's rump that she becomes invisible."

Juliet nodded. "How did Noah York take the news?"

"No idea. He wasn't in the room."

So far, this had turned out none too informative. How to learn more?

"Did Jana tell you that she'd broken off her engagement?"

Cammie held up a long section of Juliet's hair and snipped an inch off.

Juliet winced.

"I noticed she wasn't wearing her ring, but Mali was the one who told me about the breakup. She was ecstatic about it."

Juliet turned her head.

"Stay still," Cammie instructed.

"Mali was happy that Jana called off the wedding? Doesn't she like Noah?"

"Oh, she likes him. A little too much to be his cousin-in-law." She smiled in the mirror and nodded knowingly. Get it, get it, the look said.

Oh, I get it.

Juliet asked, "Cousin rivalry over the same man?"

Cammie pulled out a blow dryer with a large diffuser on the blowing end. "It wasn't just those two who fought over Noah York. Saskia…"

Teagan came back into the room with Mali right behind her. Mali said, "Makeup time. We can do your face while Cammie blows out your hair."

Wait, had Cammie meant that Saskia sneaked out of the house at night to visit Noah York?

No!

How did that work? Seriously, how many women visited Noah at night? He must keep an hourly calendar to accommodate the comings and goings of his girlfriends.

But, Saskia? Really?

Wasn't it funny that Cyril kept his cigarettes hidden from his wife when she had quite the secret herself?

Wow, Ms. Botox.

Something else struck Juliet too, what was it…?

Mali stuck a mascara wand at Juliet's eye. "Blink, blink," she instructed.

What did Cammie say?

Juliet sat up straighter. The ring! Jana wasn't wearing her engagement ring.

"Hold still," Mali complained. "Teagan, get me a makeup wipe."

"Sorry," Juliet said absently… *Before the murder Jana wasn't wearing the ring.*

No one had stolen it because she wasn't wearing it. The police thought Paris stole it; Paris thought Noah took it.

What if Jana took it off and it was in her bedroom? Had the police bothered to search the girl's belongings–and if they had, had they known where to look in the places a girl would tuck such a ring?

"Stand up, Juliet," Mali said. "Gaze upon your beauty." She stepped out of the way.

Teagan kept the camera pointed straight at her.

Juliet still wasn't crazy about the catsuit, but wow, her hair looked great. The tight curls fell more softly around her face and were less wiry than usual. The makeup wasn't bad either. Mali had applied a smoky gray shadow to Juliet's lids and highlighted them with a cream shade. Her lips were a darker red than she usually wore, but it was beautiful.

"Well," Juliet said, "I do like my hair and makeup."

"You look amazing," Mali told her. "Seriously, Juliet, you could model. Well, your face anyway. Your breasts are still far too average."

Juliet puckered her mouth and then adjusted the bra cups on the bodice of the suit.

Movement out of the corner of her eye caused her to turn toward the doorway.

Cammie spoke to someone. A tall someone with a beard.

Juliet's heart nearly jumped out of her chest.

The stylist wrote her signature electronically on a handheld device and then took a package from Paris' hand. "How'd you get in here?"

"There was no one answering, so I opened the door and found you, yeah?"

Juliet winced at the word *yeah* and glanced toward Mali and Teagan. Would they recognize Paris' phrase?

Teagan held the camera on Mali.

Mali stood in front of the fireplace. "I want you all to consider helping another human being." She pressed her hands to her heart. "I want you to feel what I feel right now. By making Juliet as beautiful as she is, has made me feel beautiful inside."

Paris gave Juliet a brief glance and moved back into the hallway.

Cammie turned to Mali.

Juliet returned to the stylist chair and, watching the mirror to see if anyone noticed her, she snatched a pair of disposable gloves from the box. There was no place to hide them in the catsuit, so she stuck them into the top of her thigh-high boot.

Slipping away, she clicked down the hallway in her boot heels. Had Paris gone to her bedroom?

Juliet took the stairs and crossed the first bridge to the other side of the house and then climbed the next set of stairs. She gazed across the expanse between the two sides of the house.

Someone on the bottom floor moved slowly with their head down. Was it one of the employees? Whoever it was wore brownish colored slacks and a white shirt.

It was Hugo, but what was he doing, searching for something? Maybe Xenia had asked where her egg went and he was pretending to look for it.

Juliet slipped quietly toward her bedroom door and opened it. "Paris?" All the way inside, she shut the door behind her. "Paris?" she whispered again, gazing toward the balcony.

Fingers touched her waist.

Juliet spun around hard and landed squarely in Paris' embrace.

He pulled her tight against him. "You look different."

She put her hands on his hard chest, feeling the muscle there. "It's Mali's butt, not mine."

Okay, it was a stupid thing to say, but Paris had startled

her. This was a murder investigation, after all. And why was she having such a hard time breathing all of a sudden?

Paris narrowed his eyes, letting her words sink in. Then he shook his head and brought his lips close to hers.

Juliet stood still, watching his lips come nearer and sinking into his embrace.

No, no, no!

She covered his mouth with her hand. This was not the time for kissing. She told him, "You're crazier than I am." Her eyes fell to his gray shirt with the smiley emblem on the breast of it. "Where'd you get an Amazon uniform?"

Paris kept a tight grip on her waist but pulled his face away from her hand. "I paid the delivery guy all the cash I had on me just to let me bring the package to the house for him. He had a second shirt in the van, so it all worked out." His green eyes wandered over her face and hair. "What have you done to yourself? You smell nice."

Juliet rolled her shoulders and pushed him away. "Focus, Paris. Do you know where Jana's bedroom is?"

"Why?"

She kept her distance, taking a breath to calm her nerves. "Because Jana took Portia's advice and broke up with Noah." With two fingers, she waved at Paris and then at herself. "We know he couldn't afford a diamond that size. The police think you killed Jana for the ring. We find the ring, and we clear you."

His fists landed on his hips, and his eyes drifted toward the ceiling as he thought it through. "Well, I can't give it to them, can I?"

"I'll give it to them," she said, dropping her hands to her side.

"And they'll say I gave it to you."

Juliet shook her head. "No. Let's just find it and then worry about how to give it to the police." She stepped toward the door, opened it, and then glanced at Paris again. "You're not allowed to touch it, though. We can't have your prints on it." Glancing left and right, she stepped into the hall. "Which way to her room?"

"It's down the hall," he said, nodding his close shaved head to the left.

A little worm of jealousy squirmed in her belly. "How do you know that?"

"Because my family visited often. Portia was always in Jana's room."

"Oh, right."

Paris took the lead and walked fast. He reached the door first and opened it very, very gently. Poking his head inside, he leaned back, and then pushed the door all the way open.

Juliet followed him inside.

The room had a slanted ceiling, white barn wood walls, and a bamboo headboard on the queen size bed. No one had gone through the area and put things away. It seemed Jana would come back any moment. Her dressing gown was on the edge of an antique quilt. Her fuzzy pink slippers had been tossed near a closet. There was no glam to the room, no abundance of mirrors and lighting, just a simple woman's place, neat and feminine. Turquoise accent furniture showed an artistic side to Jana. On a worktable along one wall were drawings and the beginning of a watercolor painting. Opposite the hearth was a gorgeous wardrobe, shabby chic style, with ornate handles and topper.

Juliet remembered the girl, vaguely. The Da Vincis and

Novaks hadn't been friends long enough that she knew Jana well. She'd been a quiet girl and certainly more likeable than Mali.

"Where do we start?" Paris asked, leaning over the dresser.

"Lock the door?"

He held up an index finger in front of his face. "Right. That's smart." He moved to the door again. "You're really good at this."

"Touch the knob with the tail of your shirt."

"Right, right," Paris told her, untucking the Amazon shirt.

Out of her thigh boot, Juliet pulled the disposable gloves, slipped them onto her hands, and then opened the first drawer of the dresser. Inside were panties and bras. The usual. It was also a spot Juliet would hide something if she wanted to keep it safe.

Pulling out the panties, she felt along the lining and the secret pocket.

"Is that a normal spot for engagement rings?" Paris wanted to know, standing next to her again.

"It's called a gusset, and some women have been known to use it for … secret things." She caught his eye. "Not me, I'm just saying."

He pulled his brows together. "Right." His eyes went to a box on the dresser. "Do you have more gloves?"

"No," she told him, as she reached forward and opened the jewelry box for him.

"Pull it closer to me."

Juliet did and then returned to her examination. So far, she hadn't found the ring. She reached farther back into the drawer.

Her hand touched something thin and plastic-like. It was hard to say what it was with gloves on, so she pulled it all the way out.

It was a plastic bag with the word Soho Gems printed across the front of it.

Juliet got excited and spilled the box out of the bag. It was a simple box, as all custom jewelry came in. She opened it and then took a long breath.

The ring was stunning, a round diamond with sapphires on the sides. Juliet lifted it toward the light coming in from the windows. The sunshine set off a burst of colors from the center stone and the halo diamonds all around it. "I'd never take this off."

Someone turned the bedroom door handle hard.

Paris grabbed her arm in alarm – which caused Juliet to drop the ring onto the rug.

The jewel hit the rug and skidded near the foot of the bed.

The doorknob rattled again, and then came the sound of a key being inserted into the lock.

Juliet's mouth fell open.

"Quick! Under the bed!"

"The ring," she said, groping for it.

Paris pushed her toward the bed. "No time!"

Oh, but she squatted for it; oh, how she missed it.

Paris had a hold of her other hand. "It's too narrow," he said and pulled her farther across the room. He ran for the wardrobe and pulled open both doors. Grabbing her arms again, Paris practically threw Juliet inside.

"Dost thou not laugh?"

Chapter 13

It was very tight inside the space.

Well, I say very...

It was ridiculously cramped inside the wardrobe because on both sides of the interior were stacked drawers, and Juliet and Paris were forced to stand in a laundry basket.

It took them a few seconds to orientate their limbs and another second to realize they'd dived in rather poorly. Juliet's face was jammed against a shelf of shoes.

Paris' elbow dug into her side. "Move over," he muttered. He was behind her, bent with his face against one of the drawers.

"I can't," she hissed. "I'll cause an avalanche."

"What?"

"Shoes," she got out.

It's so hard to breathe.

"What?"

"Shh."

No, she wasn't shushing him. Juliet had lost the ability to form words.

Noises came from outside the wardrobe, what sounded like the opening and closing of drawers.

Juliet froze.

Would the person come to the wardrobe? What if it was one of the housekeepers finally cleaning Jana's room; would they want to collect the dirty laundry that Juliet stood on top of at the moment?

Or, worse, was someone out there looking for the ring?

I could get all sorts of strangled here with these shoestrings and scarves.

Thank God there weren't any balloons in the closet!

You know who could be in the room, Juliet asked herself: Cammie. They'd literally *just* discussed Jana's engagement ring. Maybe Cammie remembered it when she'd said it and *just now* decided to find it herself. Make a little cash.

Was Cammie the killer? She'd said Noah had lots of women; was she one of them … or, was Juliet having wild thoughts because she wasn't getting enough oxygen?

All sound outside the wardrobe ceased. There came a soft clicking noise as though someone had shut the bedroom door.

Paris must've thought so too, because he moved a fraction, twisted to the right, and cracked the wardrobe door.

Then he completely fell out of it.

Juliet almost stumbled out on top of him but caught herself on the edge of a shelf. Steady again, she peeked out.

The room was empty.

Paris still lay on the floor, doubled-over, catching his breath.

In a rush to find the ring again, Juliet stepped over Paris in her six-inch boot heels and calculated her movement to land just outside of his leg.

Juliet knew right away that her calculation hadn't been successful because the left heel of the stiletto dug into muscle. It had a meaty feel to it. She swung her eyes toward Paris, her lips ready to shush him, but there was no need.

Absolutely, no need.

Paris' face registered the agony he was in; his mouth was open, his eyes just as wide, but not a sound escaped his lips.

Wow, hats off to you.

He was in complete control of the pain—except for the writhing and the bit when his hands wrapped around Juliet's ankle, and he flung her into a spin.

Juliet landed halfway on the mattress and rolled off the edge of the bed in a cartwheel position. She appreciated the speed. She fell right at the spot where she'd dropped the ring.

Yet, nothing sparkled.

"It's gone," Juliet said, sitting back on her legs. "The ring is gone … Paris?"

He'd rolled toward her, with his hands on his thigh.

"Oh my … are you okay?" She gazed at his leg. There

was no blood gushing from his wound.

He shook his head. "You skewered me," he said with ragged breath.

"I know." She patted his head. "I'm sorry." Getting to her feet, she moved toward the dresser. The Soho Gems bag was gone, and the box that had held the ring. Spinning around, she held out her hands. "Now, what do we do?"

Paris had sat up, legs crossed, the pain still evident on his features. "We find morphine."

"Be serious, will you?" she asked, trekking back toward him and taking his arm with both hands. She pulled with all her might.

He frowned at her and then put his hand on the mattress and got to his feet.

With hands placed on her hips, she said, "We needed that ring to prove you're innocent."

"I'm sure we'll find it in Noah's cottage." He limped toward the door.

Juliet followed. "Did you see him through the crack in the door?"

"No."

"Did you hear Noah's voice or something?"

Paris had his hand on the knob. "I couldn't hear anything past the padding on your butt."

Juliet gasped and placed her hands on the seat of her pants, feeling the fat batting back there. "What?"

He tilted his head. "I know your ass, and that's not it."

"*Dios Mio…*"

Paris' nose pressed against Juliet's ear. "Don't you *Dios Mio* me, woman. Now be quiet and come on."

Back in Juliet's room, Paris went to the bathroom and *presumably* checked his wound. When he came out, he sat on the chaise lounge and didn't ask her to call 9-1-1.

Juliet assumed he'd live and sat on the edge of the bed.

"Will you change out of that outfit? It's very distracting."

She gazed down at the shiny Lycra. "I think I totally am the girl to rock a catsuit and thigh boots."

"Either change your clothes or come here," he said, looking as though he meant to get up.

"I'll change, I'll change," she told him with a smile on her lips.

With the closet door closed, and the overhead light on, she selected leggings and a large white shirt. Off with the boots and on with soft ballet shoes.

Paris Nobleman—what to do about him? He was so deliciously gorgeous and funny and, in so many ways, perfect for her. He made Juliet feel so adored and wanted.

But.

She re-entered the bedroom and sat in the chair opposite the chaise, keeping her distance from him. "Better?"

"No, I still want to kiss you," he admitted, sitting forward with his elbows on his knees.

"Focus, Paris. I haven't told you that I found the green car that the florist, Yumi, described…"

"Here?"

"Yes, it's in Cyril Novak's private garage. It's a vintage Chevrolet."

His eyes stared off. "Vintage?"

"Right. Some people's *old* is another person's *vintage.*"

Off the lounger, he faced Juliet. Arms out, he said, "Then get your boyfriend to fingerprint the car."

She shook her head. "Detective Adams is not my boyfriend."

He dropped his arms. "Nicolo."

"Is not my boyfriend. You know that."

Paris' green eyes turned to slits. He moved closer to her chair and put his hands on the arms, enclosing her. "If that's true," he asked, leaning closer. "Then why won't you kiss me?"

Juliet's heart thudded hard. She didn't shy away. "Because I don't know you well enough."

He pushed off the chair as if she'd given him an uppercut to his jaw. Hand on his heart, he said, "You know everything about me."

"That's not true."

He breathed heavily through his nose with his jaw set hard. Pointing his index finger, he said, "You just can't commit to me because of Nicolo."

Juliet didn't move. "That's not true, Paris Nobleman. I won't commit to you because you keep things from me."

He leaned one shoulder back, as though she'd pushed him. "Keep things like what?" But as he said it, his mind worked over something. His brows straightened out, and his jaw slackened.

Juliet zeroed in. Off the chair, she circled him. "Why aren't you and your parents speaking to each other? Why did they cut you out of their will?"

He went back to the chaise lounge and sat. Oh, he was uncomfortable and closed off. "I can't tell you right now."

She raised her finger. "See? I don't know you."

His jawline went rigid. "I can't tell you because I'm a wanted man. Everything is screwed up, yeah?" He stuck his elbows on his knees and put his face in his hands. "I'd planned to tell you everything when you came back from Italy. I – I was so stupid."

"Is this about you loving Bexley?"

He dropped his hands to his knees and stared at Juliet. "What? No."

"Then what?"

"It's about me loving Amelia."

So many thoughts hit Juliet at once. *He met someone ... If he did, why is he coming on to me so hard? Because he wants me to help him...*

Why does my chest feel as though my heart just exploded?

Swallowing down a ball of acid, Juliet squeaked, "Who's Amelia?"

"Doing more murder in this loathsome world."

Chapter 14

His green eyes had turned a darker color. "My daughter."
Juliet sat down hard on the chair.

Paris watched Juliet closely, maybe gauging her reaction.
He said, "She was born last June."

"June?" That seemed significant for some reason.
"I met you in June. Why didn't you tell me you had a
daughter?"

"Lots of reasons." He shook his head. "I knew Bexley
was pregnant, but she thought it was Noah's."

Juliet sat up straighter. "Wait a minute, wait a minute."
She snapped her mouth shut, letting that sink in. "You and
Bexley?"

"Yes."

Juliet stared at the hearth; there was no fire now, just cold black pipes. Hugo came to her mind, and what he'd said about Saskia making Noah take a paternity test. *The baby wasn't Noah's.*

Paris didn't make any movement at all. "I…" He winced, and then continued, "I knew there was a chance the child was mine."

"Really?" she asked, her voice flat now.

He jerked one shoulder. "I thought I'd know if Amelia was mine by seeing her." He took a long breath and let it out slowly. "So, I asked Father Larry about volunteering at the orphanage."

"Father Larry? Oh." Juliet blinked. "Wait, how did you know Amelia was at the children's home?"

"I had Bexley followed."

The acid slowly filled Juliet's stomach. With every small admission from him, it ate her insides. The muscles in her jaw tightened.

He came to our home while he searched for Bexley and Amelia. Lied about his reasons for being in Verona's Vineyard. Used Matri, used me…

She said between her teeth. "When did you find out she was yours?"

"Recently."

Juliet shook her head. "What? You didn't know all this time you've been in the Vineyard?"

"I suspected she was mine." Paris wiped his face with his hand and then put his elbow on his knee. "I was scared … scared to find out that she was my daughter, and afraid that she wasn't. But then, you said something at the Valentine Ball, that Noah wasn't the father. I tried to keep my cool, but I had to take the test." He swallowed. "She's mine."

For some stupid reason, Juliet felt tears burn her eyes. "Right," she said, nodding. "And your parents don't approve?"

He shook his head. "I had decided to adopt Amelia whether she was mine or not. That's what my parents were upset about. They said to have the test, and I told them that it didn't matter. My father thinks I'm a fool, that I can't do it on my own. I turned in my stocks and bought a house."

She nodded, remembering when he came back during the Harvest Ball. She'd been so happy to see him. He'd been ignoring her texts while he'd been gone.

Juliet bent forward in her seat and hugged herself.

God, my stomach hurts. I almost fell for you…

She said, "Well, what does your father say now, you know, now that they know she's yours?"

"I haven't told them."

She flicked her eyes at the ceiling and then at Paris again. "Does Portia know?"

"Yes. She'll adopt Amelia if I go to jail."

For some reason, that hurt Juliet's heart even more. Of course, she wasn't the one to adopt the child, but … Paris had left her out of everything and every decision.

He pushed to his feet but didn't stand erect. He reached for Juliet.

She kept her hands around her middle in a hug.

Dropping his hands, he straightened. "You don't approve?"

"I approve of Amelia and that you would take responsibility for her. But *Paris*." His name came off her lips hot and seething. "You faked being in love with me to find Bexley."

He jerked his head back as though she'd slapped him. "I didn't have to fake…"

She felt a little wild right then. Off the chair, she pointed at Paris. "You did. You told my mother that you loved me so that she'd invite you to our home … so that you could snoop around the orphanage without any strings attached."

He shook his head vehemently. "I could've stayed anywhere to be near Amelia. I didn't have to stay with your family."

She took a step toward him, her anger moving her. "But it was a nice cover story, wasn't it? To keep it from your parents?"

He blinked once, his eyes very green, and he blinked once more. "Yes."

"So, you're just like Bexley."

Paris' face paled. His jaw went very rigid.

Juliet regretted her words as soon as she saw his reaction. With lips pressed together, she held her breath.

"Don't accuse me of acting like her. I didn't fall in love with your photo, of course I didn't." He jabbed his finger in the air. "You never believed that."

"Well, I'm not stupid."

"I didn't lie to your mother. I think you're beautiful. I was taken by your photo, but your mother went off the deep end over it." He shook his head. "To tell you the truth, I thought it was you who acted like Bexley. You were keeping the man you love a secret from your family."

Juliet opened her mouth, but said nothing.

He stepped closer to her. "But I started to really care

about you because you didn't use me, Juliet. You didn't fall into bed with me to fool everyone. I respected that. I didn't truly feel love for you until we were in that hallway at the church, when you were crying over Nicolo telling you goodbye. He broke your heart, but you were brave anyway." His voice softened. "I wanted to help you plant onions. That was my way of declaring my affection. I would've never helped Bexley, or any girl for that matter, plant onions …"

She shook her head, not placated. "You didn't do that much planting…"

"I went to a funeral with your cousin, who dressed like a woman."

Juliet shrugged, trying to blow that off too. As an afterthought, she stuck her hands on her waist to remain stubborn.

"I nearly killed myself getting to you when you were stuck in a closet with a killer."

She dropped her hands from her waist and then hugged her waist tightly.

"I love you. I have for so long now. I was going to tell you about Amelia and Bexley at the coffee shop."

All at once, Paris took a step backward, as though everything fell on him at once. "Then Bexley died, and I'm on the run … I was going to ask you to help me raise Amelia. I don't know what I'm going … you're the most amazing woman I know. For a while, I thought you might be too reckless, but you're not. You're brave, and you're smart…"

And then, Paris crumpled. With his head in his hands, he said, "Oh my god, Juliet. I can't have Amelia now. No one will let me take her home."

Everything he'd said pulled at her, and she reached for him. She placed her hand on his shoulder. "You'll take her home. I promise."

He gazed at her, glassy-eyed. "How?"

She shrugged. "I don't know. If Noah is the killer, let's figure it out."

"How?"

"We find the ring in his cottage."

* * *

They waited for nightfall.

Neither of them said much.

Juliet was keyed up and pacing. She watched the back lawn for anyone coming and going to Noah's place. When it was dark enough, Juliet slipped into a black jacket and returned the disposable gloves to her hands. Then she grabbed a long black sweater and took it with her to the door.

Paris grabbed the black sweater again and squeezed into it.

Literally, she could feel the sadness coming off of him. It was tangible. He moved slower and spoke slower, which reminded Juliet of her cousin, Tybalt.

But Ty is lovesick.

Was Paris? Was he really? He'd played a game when Juliet first met him. *You never really fell for that...*

Well, that was true. In front of Italia, Paris acted so in love with Juliet. But, as soon as they were alone, he didn't chase her at all. Oh yes, she'd had her suspicions back then.

But not lately.

No, even earlier that afternoon, Juliet believed

everything Paris said–because he'd proven himself over and over to be her friend. Paris Nobleman was the true-bluest out there.

He lied.

Well, so had Juliet on several occasions, and recently too. Suddenly she knew how Nicolo felt because even though she understood Paris' reasons for lying, she still didn't like the fact that he'd lied to *her*.

But here was the difference between Juliet Da Vinci and Nicolo Montague. She was not going to judge Paris right now because he was a good man. He hadn't known if Amelia was his daughter, but he was willing to adopt her anyway.

Dios Mio, he has a daughter!

Yet, even when his parents protested, and he lost the family fortune, Paris still felt a tiny little girl needed a home and was willing to step in. That was something Juliet could get behind.

It also gave her a tremendous desire to prove Paris innocent, and she pulled the bedroom door open and stepped into the hall.

Paris fell in behind her.

Juliet held up her gloved hand. "Wait here, and I'll check the hall." She took a step away from him. "I'll come and get you when it's all clear."

"I can come …"

"If I get caught, it's no big deal. If you get caught…"

He dropped his shoulders. "All right, check the hall."

She slipped away before he got the entire sentence out of his mouth. Skirting past Mali's bedroom door, Juliet rounded the bend and watched the bird. When it dipped its beak into a birdseed holder, she made her move and draped the black blouse over the cage. "Lights out, you ratfink."

She turned toward the hallway, changed her mind, and made for the doors instead. Paris would be angry with her, but it was better than going to jail for murder … yeah?

Outside, she took the stairs fast and then hurried toward the tree line, being careful to stay out of the lights. She cut across the grass at the last minute and ran toward Noah York's cottage.

God, please let Noah be out, Juliet prayed. She wanted a good look around the cottage this time. And if she didn't find the ring or some other evidence of his guilt?

Then I'll eliminate Noah and move on to the next suspect: Xenia, Cammie, Teagan, Gerald, Saskia…

Well, the list went on and on.

The shadows were deep behind the cottage. Only a small space existed between the door and the side of the main house. There was enough space for a window, and Juliet lifted herself on tiptoe to see through the parted curtains.

"Is he there?" Paris whispered.

Every nerve in Juliet's body sang a very high-pitched note. Spinning around, eyes like daggers, Juliet hissed, "Don't ever do that again."

"Don't leave without me, yeah?" he said in his usual tone.

What was wrong with him? He was far too calm … and he reached for the door handle.

Juliet smacked his hand. "Don't touch anything." Stepping in front of him, she touched the door. "Wait, why is the door open?" she whispered.

"He could be in the loft with a friend."

The thought made Juliet slow her steps a little. Noah might not be the only person in the cottage.

There was a light coming from somewhere, possibly the loft, or maybe the bathroom.

She peeked into the front room. The light definitely came from the loft. She didn't glance that direction but headed for the spiral staircase, a cement structure with carpet. Easy tiptoeing surface.

She slowed when she got eye level with the second floor. There was no one there, no feet, and no legs. Juliet glanced back at Paris. "He's not here."

"Um, yes, he is."

Juliet straightened. Had they been caught *again?* "What?"

He nodded toward the other side of the staircase.

Juliet blinked and gazed in that direction.

There was a rope tied to one of the loft rails.

She leaned further to see what was attached to it.

Oh, God, it was Noah York …

"Here's much to do with hate, but more with love."

Chapter 15

Juliet stumbled backward and grabbed the cement wall to stop her fall.

Paris caught her midway around the ribs. "Steady."

"He's dead, Paris. He's dead." The words came out in a thick tone, like she couldn't get them beyond her tongue. She couldn't take her eyes off the rope. "Why would he kill himself?"

"I don't know." He pushed her forward until her heels hit the loft floor.

There wasn't much space in the loft. A double bed fitted in the center of the one wall, the sheets all in disarray. A small dresser was tucked against the railing and the slanted roof. There was a writing desk against the other wall. That was where the lamp sat, just throwing off enough light to highlight the top. A chair was near the railing–and Noah hanging over the side of it.

Her knees wobbled hard as Juliet stumbled toward the desk. There was a pen and something next to it.

The ring! Noah had hooked the ring on the writing instrument, but why?

Juliet's eyes drifted to the papers on the desk. Noah had penned a note.

Paris read it aloud over Juliet's shoulder: "I did it. I killed Jana and the other one. I can't live with myself. My adventure ends here."

Juliet glanced over her shoulder. "He was murdered."

Paris flung out his arms. He was tall enough that his head nearly grazed the ceiling. "He just confessed to the murder."

"No, no. Something isn't right here." With her gloved fingers, she picked up the ring and stuffed it into her pocket, and then she picked up the note. Someone made it look like a suicide."

Paris shook his head. "This gets me off the hook. The police won't look for me now. I'm free." There was relief in his voice, and his eyes lit up more than the little lamp at the table.

Her eyes drifted toward the chair. "I'm not so sure about that."

Paris' brow tightened. "What?"

Juliet glanced over the railing and immediately turned away "This isn't right." She held up the note. "Noah knew Bexley's name. Why didn't he write her name?"

"Maybe he was in a hurry."

She shook the paper at him. "Bexley was killed because she saw the first murder. The killer didn't know her name."

"Juliet," Paris said, his voice dropping lower. "He did it. Noah killed them. That note," he said, pointing to her hand. "Proves it."

She shook her head. "I don't think so…"

A tapping noise sounded.

Juliet glanced at Paris.

He shot a look at the cottage door.

The tapping came louder. Someone was at the door.

Her stomach knotted. "You can't be seen here, Paris. Go." She shoved him on the shoulder. "Go!" She pushed him toward the spiral steps and followed right behind him.

They made it to the first floor.

The knock came again, and then a woman's voice said, "Noah, it's me. Open up."

Juliet ran for the back door where they had entered. Just as she turned the knob, there came the sound of keys turning in the lock at the front entrance.

She grabbed the knob. Her hand sweated too much; she couldn't turn the knob!

Paris shoved her out of the way and opened the door. He grabbed Juliet's forearm and practically threw her out the door.

Then he shut it slowly. Quietly. Pivoting, he leaned toward the window.

Juliet could barely breathe. "Who is it?"

Paris gazed at Juliet and started to say…

A high-pitched scream cut off his answer.

Juliet pushed Paris' bicep. "Run … run!"

And they did, as quietly as they could. They took a

wide berth around the side of the cottage and then ran through the trees again.

Whoever it was kept screaming.

It got louder too. Whoever it was came screaming out into the night. Tearing sobs followed, and footsteps.

Juliet got as far as the hen house and pressed her back against the wall and waited. She stuffed the suicide note into her pocket.

Paris slipped next to her. He bent close to her ear. "I saw her face when she spotted him. She didn't seem that surprised."

"What?"

Footsteps passed on the other side of the chicken coop and ran toward the house.

Juliet moved against the wall and then peeked out around the corner.

The patio was lit, and the pool threw a blue light against the walls of the house.

Mali, it was Mali running across the courtyard. She pulled open one of the French doors and practically fell into the house.

"Now is our chance," Juliet told Paris. She didn't wait for him and took off toward the patio and the stairs to the second floor.

She wrenched open the door.

Voices sounded on the first floor. Mali's mostly, still squawking and crying.

Juliet grabbed the blouse from the birdcage and bolted to her bedroom. Once inside, she spun around and waited.

Paris practically jumped into the room and then shut the door gently. He turned on Juliet, and he stared at her hand. "You have the note … why?"

Juliet dropped her eyes to the paper in her hand. "It's

fake. Someone tried to make it look like a suicide."

His green eyes flashed. "You don't know that."

It suddenly felt scorching in the room. Juliet slipped out of her coat and threw it on the bed. She still held the note in her hand. "I do know that."

He didn't say anything.

Juliet bit her lip and faced him.

Paris stood with hands on his hips, and his mouth was set in a firm line.

She said, "I know you're desperate for the police to blame Noah for the murders, but I don't think it was him." She kept her eyes on Paris, just in case he made any sudden moves. She made small steps around the bed, and when she was near the hearth, lit by one of the employees, she let the paper fall into the fire.

Paris took a step toward the hearth and pointed at the note. "I can't believe you did that." The flame in his eyes burned brighter than the one in the fireplace. His voice came out even hotter.

"Sorry, I'm sorry," she told him, holding up her hands.

His nostrils flared. Each word he said was punctuated with heat. "You tampered with evidence."

"It's the Da Vinci way, *si*?" It was her attempt to lighten his mood, which in retrospect, was a stupid, stupid thing to say.

Paris' fist landed on his hips. He still wore that ridiculously tight sweater and it accentuated his heavy breathing–like he was barely keeping control of his temper.

"We need to find the right person so that you'll never worry about going to jail again." She reached out to take his sleeve.

He jerked his shoulder back so that Juliet couldn't touch him.

"You can raise Amelia …"

Paris lifted an index finger and lowered his eyes. "Don't act like you care about her, Juliet. Don't act like you care about either one of us."

Her heart fell hard into her stomach. "I don't know Amelia yet, but I do care about you."

"Oh right," he said, letting out a bitter laugh. "If you cared about me, you would've let this ride and allow the police to figure out whether or not Noah killed himself." He threw his hands out in a wild gesture. "Now they're going to tear this place apart trying to figure out what happened. They're going to look for me."

"They might assume that it's a suicide, but we *don't* want them to stop looking for the real killer. That's what always happens, Paris."

He shook his head and lowered his voice, "What always happens, Juliet, is that you make a mistake; you choose poorly and then you get yourself into trouble." He twisted halfway toward the door. "But this time, you not only made a mistake, you put *me* in worse trouble, and you took my daughter along for the ride."

"No …" she told him, her voice breaking. It wasn't often that Juliet cried, but this was it, this was stacking up to be the moment her tear ducts meant to rival Angel Falls. "I'll fix it, you'll see."

"No, I won't see." He reached for the door handle.

"Wait," she said, rushing forward. "Wait, where will you go? You said you don't have money."

"I can't stay here, can I?" he said, waving his hand around the room. "This place will be hot in a matter of minutes."

Now the tears were coming, spilling over her bottom

lashes. "How will I find you?"

"I don't know!" He opened the door. "I've got to go."

"Meet me tomorrow…" she said, following him. "Meet me at Jinlin's."

He shook his head. "No."

"Paris?" She touched his arm.

"I'm going to find Portia. I need to find her. She'll raise Amelia." He stared at Juliet, visibly cracking as he saw the tears on her cheeks. He shook his head. "Meet me day after tomorrow. I've got to go."

She let go of his sleeve. "Okay."

He shut the door behind him.

Dios Mio, what have I done?

Juliet fell backward on the bed, arms out, and staring at the ceiling. It felt as though a weight anchored her heart to the sand in her stomach. Paris believed she'd taken away his chance to bring his daughter home.

Love me much now?

Sitting up on the edge of the bed, she let her feet dangle off the mattress. She needed to find the killer. Fast. People were dying, Paris was distraught, and someone needed to be held responsible.

Taking a deep breath, she wiped the skin beneath her eyes with her fingertips. Common sense and basic human intelligence would win this day, or maybe tomorrow, or the next day. It would happen. She'd make sure of it.

I'm not the police…

"I know I'm not the police," she chastised herself.

Off the bed, she pulled her hair into a ponytail and left the room.

* * *

There were cops everywhere downstairs and out on the lawn. Red and blue flashed on the front windows, and flashlight beams danced like fireflies in the garden outside the French doors.

Detective Adams led the charge while snapping his gum and pointing in different directions with his gloved hands. He wore a working man's suit with a dingy white shirt beneath. He'd asked the family to gather in one room and then announced Noah's death to them—as though the entire household hadn't heard Mali's screaming and figured it out already. Yes, all the theatrical gasping was a thing of the past.

Except Italia's; she gasped with Italian flair and muttered, "*Che cavolo*," which meant something along the lines of *What the he—?*

"Yesss," Detective Adams told her, his brown hair flopping in his face as he quickly turned to Juliet's mother. "We're not sure if it was suicide or not. We'd like to ask all of you to remain here while we question you individually."

Juliet sat back on the overstuffed cream-colored couch. They'd gathered in what Saskia called *the parlor*. It's where the Novak's received their visitors—or in this case, the coppers. Second time for them, right, or was their home bombarded with such occurrences? A fireplace stood at one end of the room, flames roaring, a sofa in front of a row of wrought iron covered windows, chairs opposite the couch, and a crystal chandelier hanging above them.

Mali's face wasn't visible because her hair streamed in front of it. She sat with Saskia, very close, but still on her cellphone. So much for the trauma that she'd experienced.

Saskia was dressed in a linen suit of pale blue and lacy pumps. She'd dressed for the occasion—at eleven thirty at night. Maybe that's what she'd worn to Noah's cottage earlier. Certainly, her lids were less swollen. Perhaps pushing Noah over a loft railing had opened her eyes a little wider, eh?

Juliet chewed her bottom lip. The stylist had started to tell Juliet more about the woman of the house. Was she a bit of a party animal? Saskia was never without her glass of bubbly nearby, or was it vodka from the old country?

Detective Adams gazed around the room, his eyes landing on Mali. "You're up first, Miss Novak."

Mali slumped in the chair and then rose to her feet, stuck her phone in the back pocket of her high fashioned jeans, and followed the detective.

She wasn't surprised…

Juliet gazed up at the chandelier. That's what Paris had said as Mali ran past the chicken coop; that Mali hadn't been surprised by Noah's death. What had he meant? Paris had been the one who'd seen Mali's face when the girl entered the cottage.

Maybe the girl's fortune teller had predicted the predicament and she was, like all, "Weird, but okay."

And if that was true, what was all the screaming about?

Hugo sat on the couch with Juliet, with his long legs spread out in front of him and his blonde head resting against the back of the sofa. Next to him was Gerald.

In her mind, Juliet pronounced it like *Geerralllld*. Did he visit the cottage tonight? Maybe Noah had been too friendly with Hugo, had invited him to the Outback to play one alligator, two alligators, a time too many?

Juliet peeked in the sneering man's direction. Look at him with his hair sitting on his head like a ruby red chair pouf.

When did I start to dislike Gerald so much?

It was his Billy Idol sneer and his uncommunicative behavior that turned Juliet off. No one could have an attitude like that and not be a suspect in a murder case.

Teagan was next in the lineup on the couch.

Are you still wearing a nicotine patch?

Oh, Teagan, same-samer, Mali try-harder, where was she this evening? Had she been tangled up in Noah's sheets and then decided to toss him over a railing? Was that the reason the chair was near the scene of the crime? Had she put her lover there and then shoved him over the edge?

Juliet sat up straighter. *Is that what happened?*

Had one of these ne'er do wells pushed him over and then righted the chair? The chair had still been close enough to the desk to write a fake suicide note and leave it there.

Because let's face it, no one in the room had the upper body strength to toss Noah over the rail without some help.

Juliet gazed around the room. There was Cyril, standing near the entryway, shag rug attached. Could he be the killer? He had access to the car, he smoked—albeit in the shadows—and his *I didn't know my cameras were turned off* alibi.

Next to Cyril was Xenia. Adventurous Xenia, fit as a fiddle, and ready to go scuba diving with tiger sharks at a moment's notice. Had she found her egg in the garbage disposal yet? Perhaps she'd gone to Noah's house, accused him of yolk-napping, and when he denied it, she pushed him out of the loft … and oops, watch the rope.

Yes, yes, the entire family was sketchy.

Detective Adams returned to the room, pulling in people, one-by-one. Lastly, he called Juliet.

She got to her feet and followed the detective down the hall. Suddenly, her father's voice came to her: *You don't know nothing, you didn't see nothing, and you don't say nothing.*

Juliet entered the small room beneath the first set of stairs, the one where she'd found Saskia in the throes of her Botox setback. The fireplace roared in the hearth. The custom blinds had been closed.

How intimate.

The super-hot detective from Mayville stood by the window.

Nicolo, oh Nicolo, why for art thou here, Nicolo?

Now she'd be forced to deceive him as much as she meant to mislead Adams. Juliet had to serve them a bluff sandwich because they couldn't know about the suicide note, or that Paris was anywhere near the scene of the murder.

Nicolo had his head bowed and was staring at the small notebook in his hand. He was dressed in his usual: Mayville police uniform, black polo, and khaki pants. He'd left his hair down, and it fell to his scruffy bearded chin.

Detective Adams cleared his throat.

Nicolo pushed away from the wall and came to sit on the sofa that faced the lone armchair in the center of the room.

Juliet sat in the armchair and rubbed her knees with the palms of her hands.

Nicolo's pale blue eyes landed on her and stayed there. It was as if he didn't know her at all, such was his expression. Juliet was just another witness to him.

Detective Adams asked, between gum pops, "What did you see tonight?"

"I didn't see nothing," she said with a hint of her father's accent. "Anything. I didn't see anything. I was in my room."

Adams leaned forward, his elbows on his knees. Juliet

caught a whiff of his stale aftershave. *What is that, what is that, Stetson cologne or baby powder?* He said, "I'm told you have a nice view of the lawns from your bedroom."

Huh?

"I have a good view," she confessed. This guy was a hard case.

"What'd you see?"

Juliet tipped the edges of her mouth down hard, really getting into her father's character, you know, lying. "I really wasn't paying that much attention. I was watching the *Great British Baking Show*. I love that program."

Adams sat back on the sofa, his knees spread, and with his fisted hands between his thighs. "Me too. Who's your favorite baker this year?"

Her eyes darted left fast, and then came back to his just as quickly. "Ollie," she said, making up a name, but she said it with confidence. That's what counted here.

Adams tilted his head to the side, thoughtful and disbelieving.

She explained, "I'm watching reruns. I don't know what season I'm on."

He lifted his chin. "Did you leave your room at any time this evening?"

She pretended to think about it, and then told him what she'd done last night instead. "I went and poured a glass of wine from a bottle on the kitchen counter. It triggered a gag reflex. The stuff belonged in the cellar of shame."

The detective nodded. "Any wine at room temperature is bottom of the barrel stuff." He chomped hard and snapped his gum.

Juliet eyed Nicolo.

He had a smarmy look on his face, didn't he? As if

he admired Adams and knew Juliet was in above her head here.

Adams said, "To me, Italian wines are the worst of all. They are gastrointestinal monstrosities." He held up his palms. "I know, I know, that's blasphemy, but I just can't drink them. My tongue nearly falls off."

During his little speech, Juliet had sobered appropriately and dropped her mouth wide open. She shook her head. "I can't respect you at all now."

"My loss. Did you go outside after, what did you say, gagging?"

"No."

He tilted his head, and his side sweep fell onto his brow. "I'm going to ask you again, and I want you to remember that you're not the only one in the house who has a window view of the lawn."

"They have made worms' meat out of me."

Chapter 16

Juliet's stomach knotted. "No one saw me cross the lawn, I'm sure of that, detective."

"If you didn't walk across the lawn, which way did you take to get to Mr. York's cottage?"

"I'm sorry, what?"

"Someone saw you," Nicolo said.

"I was only guessing about the window view," Adams admitted. "A witness saw you on the other side of the property this evening. So, you weren't lying, you didn't cross the lawn. You took the woods."

With her teeth clenched, Juliet leveled her stare at

Adams. "I got some fresh air after drinking the wine. No one was out there. If someone saw me, then it was the murderer sneaking back inside the house."

Nicolo rolled his eyes and sat back in the seat.

Juliet frowned at him. *How did I ever love you?*

Adams said, "Explain your statement."

"What I'm saying is that there was no one else outside when I was out there. Whoever it was that told you, that must've been the person sneaking back to the house after killing Noah."

Nicolo shook his head. "We're not sure it's murder, Juliet."

"Then why are you interviewing everybody, if it was suicide?" She had her arms on the chair rest and gripped the edges with her hands.

Adam's nodded and raised his brows. "You have a detective's mind."

"I can put things together …"

"Yes, you're a bright girl. I'm in awe." Off the sofa, he walked toward the window. He turned when he reached Juliet's side. "The witness said someone was with you. A man." He held out his hand toward Nicolo.

Nicolo handed over the notepad.

Adams flipped through the pages and then read, "The man was six foot two, had dark hair that was cut short, and had a scruffy beard and mustache." Adams' sharp eyes found Juliet's. "Were you with Paris this evening?"

"Yes," she admitted–because she had a good reason to do so.

Nicolo let out a growling sound.

She leaned forward. "That's how I know Paris is innocent. He didn't kill Noah York. He was with me all day."

"Where is he now?" Adams wanted to know.

"He left."

"Excuse me for a moment," Adams said and removed a cellphone from his pocket. He turned away from Juliet and told whoever answered the phone, "Change the BOLO on Nobleman to short brown hair, beard, and mustache."

Juliet's nerves zinged with every descriptive word the detective uttered.

Adams returned his cellphone to his pocket and stood again. "Thank you, Miss Da Vinci. You've been cooperative and helpful."

Juliet used the chair arms to pull herself out of the chair. "Don't you want to know what I've learned?"

"Not particularly." Adams stuck his hands in his trouser pockets. "I don't like people like you, Miss Da Vinci. You think you can figure things out on your own. You get your hands into it, and all you do is muddy the waters for the professionals." His gaze looked her up and down, and then he straightened. "You can go now." He moved toward the door and held out his hand.

Juliet stared at Nicolo.

He didn't return her gaze. Nicolo's eyes were on Adams.

* * *

Back in her room, Juliet paced in front of the fireplace.

Who'd seen her and Paris outside—Mali? No, she'd been too busy screaming and running.

Teagan?

Juliet stopped pacing. Teagan had seen her two nights ago sneaking back from Noah's cottage … had she seen Paris, too, and was just now telling the detectives about it.

You're not the only one with a good view of the lawn.

What other bedrooms had a look at the garden, especially the trees where Juliet had run through?

Her bedroom was the only one on this side of the house with a view overlooking the lawn. Whoever the star witness was lived on the other side of the house.

Hugo's room was there. Presumably, Cyril and Saskia's suite was located there, as well.

Juliet slipped out into the hallway.

Mali's windows faced south. So did Jana's room.

She crept down the hall toward the birdcage.

Directly on the floor beneath her, was Cyril's office. His windows faced the lawn–but not the trees.

The spa, movie theater, and the vintage car garage were all on the first floor.

Someone in the spa wing might've seen us.

But was anyone in the spa at nine thirty or ten o'clock?

Juliet shrugged, went down a flight of stairs, and crossed the bridge. She'd never been in this part of the house. Along the hall, there was a bank of windows. They faced the courtyard, not Noah's cottage, no, but a bit of the tree line…

She leaned closer to the window. How good would the witness's eyesight have to be to describe Paris so well at that distance?

The bottom floor was the kitchen and dining area and all the French doors. That wasn't a good view, though; it'd be easier to see from the second and third stories.

Juliet turned, meaning to head to the third story.

Someone blocked her path. Someone in a black polo shirt …

Nicolo's blue eyes watched Juliet, taking in her

oversized shirt and ballet shoes. He'd leaned against the wall, just waiting for her to turn around, apparently. "You hid Paris? Here?"

Che cavolo! Juliet thought, and then explained, "I wouldn't call it hiding him. He was here and stayed one night."

"Juliet!" The disapproval was like a fireball directed right at her.

She wrinkled the bridge of her nose. "Paris stayed on the couch, Nicolo."

"You knew I was looking for him."

"I did tell him that you wanted to speak to him. You weren't going to arrest him, right? It's not as though I was harboring a fugitive."

He stood up straighter and held up his index finger. "I will tear this house apart…"

"I swear to you, he's not here."

Nicolo's eyes darted toward the window and then back to Juliet. "Don't take it personally, but I don't believe you." His gaze went to the window again. "What were you looking for? You had your nose pressed pretty hard against the glass here."

She moved toward the window and gazed out again, where the lighting hit the ferns and the trees. "Adams said someone saw me from a window. I'm probably mistaken…"

"You are."

She raised her brows and leaned away from him.

"I'm just saying."

"I don't remember any windows on this side of the house. This one doesn't even have a direct view of where I was standing." She faced Nicolo again. "I'm telling you, it was the killer who saw me."

He faced the window and gazed toward the trees.

"The witness didn't say they saw you from their bedroom window. Adams set you up with that question."

"Did he?" Juliet asked. "Or did he set me up by saying he was only kidding? I don't like him."

Nicolo barked a laugh. "I'll bet you don't. He's a decorated officer, Juliet. A keen detective."

"That's not the reason I dislike him, you know, since I'm not a criminal."

"Then why don't you like him?" He turned from the window and held her eyes. "Because he thinks faster than you?"

She winced. "No."

"Then what is it?"

Juliet lifted her chin. "He pops his gum. I hate that. Does he chew gum all the time? Every time I see the man, he's at it." Juliet leaned her shoulder on the glass. "And what sort of gum does he chew, bubble wrap? It's not just one pop with him, but five pops per chew. What is it, rock candy gum? Firecracker wad? I can't get that kind of snap out of Wrigley's."

Nicolo stared at her. "I … I don't know."

"What's wrong, Nicolo, not as fast a thinker as I am?"

His features fell. Before he could come up with anything clever to say, someone else came around the corner of the wall.

Xenia took a step backward. "Oh, hello." She held out her hand. "Sorry if I interrupted your conversation."

Nicolo shook his head. "I need to join the others." He touched Juliet's arm. "I'll talk to you later. And, I'll let you know about the brand of gum when I find out what it is."

"Yes, fine," she told him, playing along. "I'm interested to know."

Xenia took a couple of steps to stand next to Juliet and

then stared out the window. She had a darker complexion than her brother, Cyril. Her hair was very full–also unlike Cyril's. Perhaps he'd been a brunette before the rug landed on his head. "The detective is handsome. How do you know him?"

She gave Xenia a side smile. "He's arrested a couple of people I know."

The woman gave a slow nod. "That makes you either a criminal or a police officer."

"Neither," Juliet told her, gazing at Xenia's reflection. "Detective Montague is assisting the Erie police. He's involved because the second murder happened in Mayville, NY. We're both from the same area."

"I see," Xenia said. "I wonder how Noah died. Did your detective say?"

"He's not actually *my* detective." Juliet wanted to make that perfectly clear. To everyone.

"I mean, in the sense that the detective is from your world of Mayville."

"Oh, I see. Well, Nicolo didn't tell me how Noah died."

Xenia faced Juliet. She was much taller, at least five foot eight to Juliet's five foot four. She said, "He'll be mourned, of course, but we all saw it coming, and he kind of deserved it."

"You think someone killed him then? The detectives think it might've been suicide."

Xenia let out a laugh–or what might've been a laugh. It was just a weird sound, and then she said, "You don't believe that, do you? Noah was too much of a hedonist to kill himself."

"But, who killed him … I mean, in your opinion?"

She raised her thin brows. "Other than you?"

Um, whoa?

"I believe your detective, and the other fellow, the gum chewer, they think any one of us might be the murderer." Her dark eyes looked Juliet up and down. "He certainly thought I was. I suppose everyone's capable, given the right circumstances." She held up her hand and ticked off the list. "Money, revenge, or mental instability …" She nodded at Juliet with her last point. "Jealousy."

"I'm not jealous."

She tilted forward. "Let's stop talking about you for a moment."

Juliet snapped her mouth closed.

Xenia continued, "In this case, I believe it was jealousy that killed Noah York. And I think a man in this house is responsible."

"You think your brother did it?

Xenia's forehead wrinkled, "Cyril is not the only man in this house."

"Hugo then?"

She rolled her hand. "Keep going. They aren't the only men who live here."

"Gerald?"

Xenia lifted a shoulder.

"It could be a woman."

"They usually work with poison, so I understand."

Juliet let out a small laugh. "Men kill with poison, er, I happen to know."

Xenia took a long breath through her very straight nose. "All right, I'll play along. Which woman?"

"You, for one."

She smiled, showing uneven teeth in the front. Juliet had never noticed that about her until this minute. They weren't pearly white teeth either.

Smoker?

Xenia nodded. "Yes, I could've done it. I didn't like Noah York. I'm sure you've heard me say so. But I wouldn't have taken a hammer to him."

"We don't know how he died," Juliet reminded her.

"Yes, I'm assuming someone took a hammer to him. My motive would be revenge."

"Why?"

"Because he killed Jana."

Juliet leaned back, the side of her arm brushing the window. "You know that?"

"No, I didn't see him do it if that's what you mean, but I was pretty sure he did." She bit the side of her lip, seemingly thinking it through. "His death has put a hole in the idea. I thought Noah killed Jana because of the other woman who died. Hexley somebody…"

"Bexley Pemberton-Kerr."

Xenia didn't care what Bexley's name was; it was evident by her curled upper lip. "Noah knew them both. He was the link in the murders– my opinion."

"The police questioned him," Juliet reminded her.

"Many times."

Juliet threw out her next guess, "Why would Saskia kill them?"

Xenia jogged her head back and forth. "Jealousy."

"She was having an affair?"

"I don't *know* it for sure, but if it was a woman who did the killing, and jealousy was the motive, then Saskia isn't the only suspect. Mali and Teagan and Cammie had relations with Noah, too."

Juliet pursed her lips in thought. "Why did Noah ask

Jana to marry him then?"

"Because Jana was the most innocent of the group. I doubt she knew that he slept with everyone. She was the most wide-eyed of them all and was willing to trust him with her fortune. All the other ladies were wise to Noah York's ways."

"Hugo told me that you brought Noah here. Did you?"

Her eyes twitched–just a little bit, as if the information surprised her. "Hugo said that?"

"Did he get it wrong?"

Or did he lie?

"No, no," she answered, sounding like a protective aunt. "He's right. I met Noah while jumping out of an airplane." She turned toward the stairs.

Juliet followed her. "That's funny, Hugo thought you pulled Noah out of a volcano."

Xenia laughed; it sounded nervous. Too high.

"Yes, Hugo is right. The plane was named Volcano." She called over her shoulder, descending the steps quickly.

Juliet got to the second landing and watched Xenia speed to the first floor.

A plane named Volcano? Oh yeah, that all checked out.

* * *

Juliet barely slept, and when she did, it was on the chaise lounge and not the bed. She dreamed of Paris. He ran from her and she chased him until she saw Madame Olei standing in front of the Jinlin's Dine-In. "You will chase the man you love," she said over and over.

Love Paris?

Juliet threw off the blanket, rather roughly, showered

and changed into another one of Mali's outfits. Juliet was really beginning to miss her wardrobe while choosing a pair of leather pants and a black off-the-shoulder sweater.

She was near the second story landing when she heard voices. Pausing on the step, Juliet bent low to listen to the conversation.

"I told you he was trouble."

Juliet recognized Xenia's voice and bent lower, trying to see the woman. It was no use. The wall was in her way.

A man's voice said, "What trouble? He killed himself. How does that affect you?"

"It affects everyone, Cyril. Look around you. Death has touched everyone in this house, beginning with sweet Jana. Have you forgotten about her?"

"Of course I haven't forgotten Jana," Cyril snapped. "What a thing to suggest. I'm only saying Noah York wasn't the cause of the trouble in this house."

"You're right about that," Xenia said, her voice fading. "There was trouble in this house long before anybody died."

A door slammed shut.

Juliet stood straighter and waited a moment before taking the remaining stairway to the first floor.

The dining room smelled of cinnamon rolls and weak coffee.

Mali and Hugo sat at one end of the long dining table, eating their breakfasts beneath the chandeliers, but not speaking. Behind them and through the bank of windows, the sun shone down on the police officers walking the grounds with their badges winking in the twinkling light.

Italia and Saskia sat at the center of the table, on the same side of it. They kept their heads together, discussing something.

Juliet went to the breakfast station and gazed at the coffee in the pot in the machine.

Gag.

She really needed to find the killer so she could get out of here and find a decent cup of coffee to drink. Maybe she'd drive to that coffee shop…

Drive… I need to drive today.

"Some shall be pardon'd, and some punished"

Chapter 17

Mali was at the table. The girl didn't speak to Juliet, but to her camera phone. Where was her fancy camcorder? "I'm not eating much this morning," she told her Instagram and Twitter followers. "I'm in mourning again."

Where was Teagan?

Juliet twisted around and checked the attendance at the table again. Gerald was missing too.

Suddenly Juliet's mother sidled next to her at the breakfast bar. "I'm going to call your father and tell him I'm staying for another week."

Juliet leaned away from her. "Why?"

Italia wore another new outfit this morning–one that included white fur along the collar. Where was she going, the arctic? "Saskia's just sick over all of this. Noah's death has punctuated the fact that she's recently lost Jana."

Juliet doubted that very much, but she nodded. "Right." She turned again and gazed at Saskia.

The woman's features were pallid, more than usual. She'd left her blonde tresses down as well, and wore blood red lipstick. It was like looking at a blonde Morticia Addams. Saskia had even dressed in black. Juliet told her mother, "At least her eyelids are less swollen."

Italia nodded. "Still looking a bit Asian, though."

Juliet gasped. "*Matri*!"

"What?" she asked, micro bladed brows going sky high. "She does look pale."

Juliet's shoulders dropped in relief. "You said ashen?"

"Yes, why? What did you think I said?"

"Asian."

"Juliet, really. This is no time for joking." Her eyes went to Mali and Hugo at the dining table. "Don't say anything like that in front of Hugo. He'd be insulted."

"I didn't get much sleep last night," Juliet defended.

Her mother pushed her on the shoulder. Hard. "Go comfort the dear boy. He looks shattered."

With such a push, Juliet stumbled toward the table.

Hugo was nearest to her. He had a plate of eggs in front of him, but only rearranged them with his fork instead of eating them. He did have a shattered air about him.

Juliet sat on the other side of him. "Are you okay?"

He dropped the fork and turned droopy eyes on her. "Gerald and I have had an argument."

"What about?"

He leaned toward her and lowered his voice, "Sergeant Mommy's purse strings."

Juliet gazed out toward the lawn again and then out the French doors and courtyard beyond. "Where is he?"

He shook his white-blonde head. "He stormed off somewhere."

"Oh," she said, putting her arm on the table and shifting toward him.

Juliet nodded toward Mali. "What's going on over there?"

Before Hugo answered, Saskia got out of her seat, and went around the back of Mali's chair. "Why don't you get that camera out of your face for one minute?" She kept walking toward the coffee pot on the other side of the room.

"Thank you," Mali called over her shoulder. "You just ruined my post." The girl set the phone on the table and glanced in Juliet's direction. She was dressed in a sleeveless blouse that revealed a remarkable amount of cleavage.

She looks good.

Juliet leaned toward the girl. "Where's Teagan?"

"She left," Mali said. Out of her seat, she turned toward the outer room and staircases.

Hugo said, "I'm thinking about leaving myself. Want to come?"

Juliet got out of her seat, too. "Where?"

"The zoo."

"The zoo?" she asked.

"I like the exhibits. Do you want to go?" Hugo shoved his plate toward the center of the table.

"No thanks, I think I'll take a drive," she told him,

getting to her feet.

"Where?" Hugo asked, standing too.

"Your dad offered to let me borrow one of the vintage cars. I think I'll take him up on it."

"Maybe Xenia will go with me then."

* * *

After returning to her room for the disposable gloves, Juliet found Cyril in his office.

He had his back to her and stared at a computer screen. "What is it?" he asked over his shoulder.

"Just wondered if I could borrow the vintage Chevy. I'd like to take it around the estate. I feel a little stuck inside today."

He turned, smile fixed in place–which was better than the toupee on his head, which was not set in place. He needed carpet glue. He said, "You girls. That's not just a green Chevy. It's a 700 Club Coupe Corvair 145 Super Turbo-Air."

"Okay, but can I borrow it?" she asked, shifting her weight.

He put his arm on the back of his seat and turned farther toward her. "You do realize that there's a 1937 Rolls-Royce Phantom III out there?"

"I do," she said, nodding. "And it's gorgeous."

His brows dropped. "You don't know which one it is, do you?"

Oh, he was one of those car sticklers, was he?

Juliet guessed, "The maroon one?"

Cringing, he got out of the chair and pulled keys out of his pocket. "I'll have you know its Tudor Metallic Red."

Yeah, well, close enough Professor.

He pulled open a drawer and took out the metal key case.

She leaned her hip against the desk. "May I borrow the green one?"

"You're just like Mali," he told her, pulling a key from the box and putting it in her hand.

She squeezed her fingers over the key. "In what way?"

"It's her favorite car, too."

Juliet stood, ready to leave. "I can't imagine Mali driving it at all."

"It usually has something to do with her damn camera," he said, falling back into the seat.

"She vlogs about the car?"

"I think she takes photos of herself inside of it." He wiggled the mouse. "I wish I could join you for a spin around the property, but I've got a conference call to make."

She headed for the door. "I'll bring your keys back soon."

* * *

Juliet wasn't sure what to do once she got to the garage. How did she drive out, for instance? She remembered that the doors had louvers on them, but did she need to push a button …? Maybe there was something like a garage door opener inside the car.

The Chevy was parked in the same position as the last time Juliet examined it. Climbing into the driver's seat, well, she felt like a kid. Everything inside was compact and a little squished. She turned the ignition, gripped the huge steering wheel, and pulled forward.

When the car was halfway down the ramp, the glass doors moved. It was supermarket machinery, apparently.

She pressed the accelerator, and she was off, down a gravel drive, and toward a forest of trees. She sat up high in the seat and held on. The steering wheel felt loose. Even when she turned it, there was hesitation to it.

Suddenly she felt as light and bouncy as the seat beneath her. The sun was high, and it hit the top of the trees and sent beams down onto the brown undergrowth.

Juliet cracked the window. Cold air seeped inside and smelled of pine needles and wood smoke. Once she'd driven a mile from the house, she pulled off the path and shut off the engine. She wasn't sure what to look for exactly. Still seated, she ran her hand along the seat, feeling for anything that the killer might've left behind.

She sniffed the interior again, trying to detect the smell of cigarette smoke.

There was nothing.

Bending, she looked beneath the bench.

The car was clean.

Juliet opened the glove box and then shut it; she noticed her hand shook when she pulled it away from the dashboard. Clasping her fingers together, she rubbed her hands. Her nerves were frayed.

I'm getting desperate, she told herself.

Think!

But, it was hard to think, knowing how upset Paris was with her. Where was he? Were he and Portia heading for the Canadian border?

No, he said he'd meet her at Jinlin's. Paris wouldn't leave without her. Right?

Biting her lip, Juliet got out of the front seat and opened the back door of the Chevy.

The seats were just as clean as the front seat. Juliet ran her fingers between the bench cushions … nothing.

Juliet sat there a moment, letting her attention drift from the seat to the floors…

Wait.

Bending forward, she pulled at a piece of white … plastic? Her gloved fingers slipped, and she tried again. Whatever it was had remained between the seat and the chrome piece running along the bottom.

Juliet pushed the seat forward and pulled at the plastic again.

It came out in her hand.

It was a badge of some sort. Across the top of it: Housekeeping.

Her frayed nerves untangled a few more threads. Juliet breathed heavier and turned the card over. There was a scannable image and then at the bottom: Porta di Messa Hotel.

A thrill shot through her, and Juliet jumped and hit her head on the interior roof of the car.

This was it! This was the evidence she needed. Jamming it into the pocket of her leather pants, she hopped out of the car, and then into the front seat again. "I found it, I found it," she said, and then repeated it under her breath as she started the car.

Making a U-turn, she punched the accelerator.

The Chevy responded like Tommy-gun-toting bandits were chasing it. It peeled out, burned rubber, and sprayed gravel out behind it.

I want one of these!

It only took ten minutes to return to the garage. The glass doors opened automatically, and Juliet pulled the Corvair into its spot. She checked the badge again and then put her hand on the window crank to roll up the glass.

Then she stopped.

There came a ticking sound.

Yes, the car engine, but there was something else.

Juliet gazed at the other cars in the garage, the pendant lights hanging from the ceiling … the shiny floor.

Foreboding. That's what it was, a foreboding was making Juliet's shoulders bend together. Something wasn't right.

Or maybe it was just *déjà vu*. It'd been two days since she'd been in the garage, and the last time someone threw a wrench at her.

Were they back? Did a deformed and bitter phantom haunt the garage?

Juliet felt eyes on her, and it made the hair on the back of her neck stand up. She sat in the car, waiting. Watching.

I'm just paranoid. I have proof someone took this car and was at the Porte di Messa, and now I think someone will try to kill me.

She let out a small laugh.

Classic me…

Besides, she couldn't sit in the car forever.

Juliet pulled the door lever and slipped out of the Corvair. Pressing the door shut as softly as she could, she then ducked behind the Chevy.

She waited again. Bending at the waist, Juliet angled to the left, to watch for movement beneath the next car.

There was no one there.

Straightening, she stepped off the platform in a ladylike movement … and then flat out ran to the house door.

Okay, she'd made it to the hall without getting murdered.

Good for me.

Refusing to look behind herself again, Juliet rushed up the first set of stairs, ran through the hallway, and opened Cyril's door without knocking.

He was on a Zoom meeting. There were at least ten people on the screen in front of him.

Juliet crept forward, mouthing *sorry* to Cyril and laid the keys on his desk. She turned and tiptoed toward the door. But then, she paused.

Just to her left was the closet that housed the security cameras. Sure, she wanted to see if someone was out in the hall stalking about, waiting for her to emerge.

Juliet slid to the left and then glanced over her shoulder at Cyril.

He still stared at the computer screen.

With a deep breath, she reached out and pulled the cabinet door open.

There was all the surveillance equipment, just as they'd been the other day, with several monitors.

They were all black again.

I'll just wiggle the mouse…

Wait. There was no mouse.

She hit the space bar on the keyboard.

Nothing. All the screens remained black.

Juliet backed away. Okay, so either the security program went down again–which she had a hard time believing, or, someone had turned the cameras off again—just in time to murder Noah York.

She glanced over her shoulder at Cyril.

His eyes were right on Juliet. And his eyebrows met

in the middle of his face like a wild furry worm. Was he thinking about what someone on the computer had said, or was Cyril thinking about how he'd strangle Juliet later?

Swallowing hard, she hurried toward the door and practically jumped into the hallway … just in time to see someone's backside flit around the wall at the end of the hall. Someone with ruby red hair.

Gerald!

Juliet hurried forward, hoping to see Gerald on the stairway or the bridge. She got as far as the railing.

"Miss Da Vinci," someone shouted up to her from the first floor. It was a female voice.

She leaned forward enough to see the first level of the house, the shiny floors, and a woman standing next to a box on the wall. It was one of the staff women Juliet usually saw in the kitchen. She was a compact little thing, chubby, and gray-haired. "You have a telephone call."

Juliet frowned. "I do?"

"Yes." She held out the receiver.

"Thank you," she said, taking the stairs.

The cook had already returned to the kitchen when Juliet reached the phone. "Hello …?"

Anthony Yeager didn't bother to introduce himself on the other end of the line. As the Da Vinci's estate manager, he probably assumed Juliet would recognize his voice. He said, "A woman called the house asking for you. She said she was on a public phone so the police wouldn't trace her."

Huh?

He continued, "The caller ID was GetGo of Erie."

Out of the corner of her eye, Juliet saw a flash of ruby red hair. She whipped around and kept her back to the wall.

Anthony said, "She said her name was Portia."

Juliet nearly dropped the receiver. "That's Paris' sister!"

"Correct," Anthony said. "Apparently, Paris was supposed to meet her last night but never showed up."

Juliet's stomach hit the floor. "He's missing?" she asked, her mouth suddenly dry.

"That is her opinion, yes."

Her nerves buzzed like an old telephone wire. Juliet could almost hear them zinging through her body. Do the police have him? No, Nicolo would've said something.

Maybe the killer found him before he left the property? Was Paris out on the lawn somewhere with a goodbye kiss balloon around his neck…?

Snap out of it! Paris is fine. He has to be okay.

"Juliet?" Anthony asked.

"Oh, sorry," she said, trying to focus. "Will you call her and ask her to meet me at the Jinlin's Dine-In tomorrow at noon?"

"You're making that up," he said in the same tone he always used. Anthony used little emotion while speaking–unless he was being accused of murder. Then his voice went slightly higher.

"It's a restaurant."

"Sounds classy."

"Oh, it is. And it has an ATM inside. I need to get Paris some money."

"Right. Goodbye," Anthony said and hung up.

Juliet replaced the receiver and shut the box door.

Where is Paris?

Had he tried to get to Portia, seen the police hanging around, and backed off? Were the police following her, too, to get to Paris? Surely, they were, if she thought to use a landline instead of a cellphone. Portia was being watched.

Which meant they'd follow Portia to the Jinlin's…

Juliet turned toward the phone again to call Anthony, to stop him from telling Portia to meet her.

The smell of cigarettes hit her nose and Juliet half turned around.

"It is my lady, O, it is my love!
Oh, that she knew she were!"

Chapter 18

"Hey," Gerald said, with his nose up and his chin out. He'd hooked his thumbs on the belt loops of his jeans. He wasn't an overly big man and was built like a swimmer, long through the torso. "Stay away from him."

Juliet took a step back with the phone receiver paused midway to her ear. "Who?"

"Don't play stupid." It was impressive that he could sneer and speak at the same time. Distracting, even. "You know who."

"Hugo?" she guessed. But, obviously, he meant Hugo

because Gerald and Juliet didn't run in the same circles. Oh, heck no. The only friend Juliet had in the hood was Abram, and he didn't count because Abram wore elevator boots.

Gerald's eyes darted away and then came back. Nodding, his shoulders bobbed with the same rhythm. "He told me he's going to marry you."

Juliet hadn't hung up the phone, thinking the receiver was enough of a weapon to work Gerald over if he tried anything. She'd widen his teeth a little, because frankly she wasn't in the mood for this conversation. "I'm not marrying Hugo."

He slid closer, still rocking his body like Busta Rhymes. "That's not what he said. He said you're thinking about it and that you're a traditionalist who wants babies."

"No, no, no … did Hugo say that?" She waved the phone piece at him. "None of that is true," she told him, and then recanted, "except the traditionalist part, and having babies bit. But, I don't want to do that with Hugo."

He raised a finger in her face. "I don't believe you. Everyone lies in this house." Dropping his hand, he nodded over his shoulder. "Little Hugo is so easily swayed. You'll want him to act like a true husband, and he'll oblige just to please you. He's a pleaser, my Hugo." He took a deep breath through his flaring nostrils. "Mommy's little boy. But, he's not going to be anybody's little boy if he keeps it up."

At the beginning of this conversation, Juliet's face had gone into a cringe. So far, she hadn't dropped the expression. "What does that mean?"

He shrugged and looked her up and down at the same time. "Don't worry about it. Just stay away from him."

He turned toward the staircase as though nothing had transpired between them.

"*Cretino*," Juliet said and turned toward the phone again. She dialed home and waited.

"Juliet?" Anthony asked on the other end of the line.

"Did you already speak to Portia?"

"I did."

She winced. "What's the phone number she called from?"

"Hang on," he said.

Juliet pulled the burner phone out of her pocket and waited.

"814-555-1374."

"Got it, thanks." She hung up and dialed the Get Go.

After ten rings, she hung up. Portia had long gone.

Juliet was a bundle of nerves climbing the stairs to her room.

Where are you, Paris?

Her chest hurt, and she rubbed the muscle above her bra. Should she look for Paris outside on the property, drive out in the neighborhoods, and search the alleys for him? Maybe she should go hang out at the GetGo and watch for Portia.

I don't even know what Portia looks like…

Nicolo was probably hiding in the bushes outside anyway, just waiting for Juliet to make a move toward Paris.

Opening the bedroom door, she went straight to the balcony and leaned on the railing. The pool below smelled heavily of chlorine, as though it had just been treated. But there was a top note above the chlorine. It was a Gerald smell … cigarettes, and regret.

Juliet leaned farther over the railing. *Where are you, stalker boy?* He was a peculiar mystery, wasn't he, and much higher on Juliet's suspect list now. Had he warned Noah to stay away from Hugo, and when Noah laughed at him, Gerald pushed him into a chair, put a rope around his neck, and then shoved him over the rails?

The only problem with the theory was that Gerald wasn't blonde. Yes, there was the wig idea, but where would a thug like Gerald get a wig—at Snatching Wigs, or the Fistful of Doll Hairs?

Juliet laughed at her own joke and then rubbed her eyes.

Dios Mio, I'm tired.

She returned to the bedroom and fell onto the bed backward. Before she got too comfortable, she twisted onto her side and pulled the disposable gloves from her back pocket and fit them onto her hands. Then, she pulled the Porta di Messa badge from her other pocket. She only touched the edge of it.

There were prints on the badge, vague marks … the killer's fingerprints?

Rolling over again, she pulled the phone from her pocket and snapped a photo of the badge. She meant to message it to Nicolo. The police needed to know about the badge. It was firm evidence that the killer used the Corvair downstairs.

Juliet stared at the screen for fifteen seconds before her tired brain realized that Messenger wasn't pulling up on the phone.

Too sleepy to think about it, she put it on the bedside table, slipped the badge into her pocket again, and removed the gloves. She'd figure it out after a nap.

Leaning back again, she ran through it all again in

her exhausted brain. The killer was blonde, *maybe*, and borrowed the Corvair to wait for Jana outside the Jinlin's. After the business with the balloons, the killer saw Bexley run from the scene and then followed her.

But why kill Noah?

To make Noah look guilty of murder and have the police stop searching for the real killer?

Right. Because the person left a fake note, all of which made Juliet think about Paris again and how mad he'd been when he'd left the bedroom.

Juliet's heart hurt again, and she rolled onto her side, fluffed a pillow, and then dropped her head onto it.

The note *was* a fake because, firstly, why would Noah steal the ring from Jana's room just to place it on top of a suicide note? That made no sense. He wouldn't try to find the ring. No, he'd write the letter, name Bexley as the second murder victim, and fall straight over the side to his death.

* * *

Juliet slept for hours. When she woke, the sun was already on the western side of the house and setting fast. Her room was semi-dark with long shadows coming from the north window and shooting toward the hearth.

She sat up and looked at her clothes. She was still in the black sweater and leather pants. They'd turned out to be great pajamas.

Rolling off the bed, she picked up the phone from the bedside table. No wonder Messenger hadn't worked. She'd tried to send the photo of the badge with the burner phone. She set it on the table again and moved across the room to find her purse. It was on a chair near the French doors.

Something thumped onto the floor.

At first, she thought it was the phone falling off the table and turned around.

The phone was still on the table.

The sound came again, but Juliet had been mistaken. The noise came from beyond the bedroom door. Juliet saw the knob twist …

So did her insides.

Immediately, she dove for the bed, crouched beside it and waited. She didn't breathe.

There was no sound.

Had she imagined the knob turning?

Juliet bent farther and peeked under the bed. No use, the blankets hung off the side.

She was too scared to glimpse over the bed, so she lay flat on the floor and scooted underneath the bedframe.

Pulling herself forward, gently, carefully, she reached the opposite side of the bed and lifted the blanket with her fingertips.

Nothing. No one was there.

Still, she lay there, waiting.

Something scraped the bedside table.

Juliet squeezed her eyes shut, willing herself to remain still.

The bedside drawer opened.

Easing herself on to her side, as much as she could, Juliet gazed toward the direction of the sound.

Boots. She saw them, the backside of them anyway, just the heel part. They were black and mid-height.

What had Gerald been wearing? Had he been in the

garage earlier, did he know she had the badge?

The boots took a step toward the French doors, toward her purse.

A hot, bitter taste filled her mouth. Where had she left the badge?

Where did I leave it?

Wait, it was in her back pocket.

Now, how to see who was in the room with her, you know, without getting all sorts of strangled.

The boots moved toward the end of the bed, toward the closet.

Juliet bent in half. She lifted the blanket…

Whoever was there had a penlight, and they pointed at the clothes, onto the shelf, then onto the floor.

The clothes moved in jerky motions as the person searched pockets.

Juliet's breath came faster. It was hard to stay so still, on her stomach, and breathe with ease.

Suddenly the person stepped out of the closet. Evidently, they didn't feel the need to stay cautious. More drawers opened, panties fell onto the floor. Shoes skidded across the floor.

One skidded in front of Juliet's face.

She wanted so badly to act bravely and crawl from beneath the bed. Face the killer! What she did instead was scoot to the head of the bed and lie there frightened. Yes, she was a by-God Da Vinci, but there was a serial killer in her room, and they probably had a rope stuffed into their back pocket.

The bed moved, and the blankets lifted…

Juliet flattened herself against the headboard wall and closed her eyes. She held her breath.

And waited.

And waited some more.

A clicking sound came from the doorway.

They're gone.

It still took her another couple of minutes to get out from beneath the bed. When she did, she slipped forward, locked the door, and turned on the light. Then she turned and surveyed the room. There were clothes on the floor, and her purse had been emptied onto the dresser. She glanced at the bedside table. The burner phone was gone.

Well, that just showed how much the killer didn't know. Juliet felt the outline of the badge in her back pocket. "I've got the badge and another phone Mr. or Mrs. Psycho."

Her hands were still shaking, and she sat on the chaise. The question now was what to do. Obviously, she'd speak to the police.

But when?

If she called Nicolo now, he'd come to the house right away. He might be right outside the front door for all she knew.

No, Juliet needed to time this just right. She'd meet Portia and Paris, make sure they had money, and then she'd go to the police with all the evidence she had.

Right.

In the meanwhile, she just needed to get through one scary night in this bedroom, and then she'd be off.

She didn't clean the mess the intruder made. It was evidence. She did, however, pick up a wrought iron lamp and hold it in her lap. She left the lights on and turned up the fireplace. Yes, Juliet had settled in for a long night.

* * *

Surprisingly, Juliet slept. When she woke, the lamp was on the bed next to her. It was a good thing the killer hadn't returned during the night. That's right, they would've met her smiting stick. She picked up the lamp and waved it. "Say hello to my little friend." Yes, it was her club of sunshine.

How brave she was in the daytime.

Changing into jeans and long leather jacket, Juliet took the second story exit, crossed the back garden, and then hiked the woods toward the fence at the road. The police were everywhere. They'd follow her if she took the Fiat.

It felt as though she was on a two-day expedition.

She heard traffic past the iron fence. Juliet threw a stick at it, just in case it was plugged in. Nothing blew up. Shrugging, she moved forward. Finally, she found a spot she could work with, a light pole.

Now, why anybody hadn't figured out to do this in the past was a mystery. The poles had ladders built right into them. Juliet climbed to the top of the fence.

Oh, that's why no one has tried this.

There were stakes on the other side of the pole, and it was a twelve foot drop. Well, there was nothing to do, but …

No, she wasn't going to jump it. What she did was grab onto the pole and straddle it. In somewhat of a hurry, she slithered down a bit and then held onto the iron fence. Then she let go.

Oh, it was a drop. The pole helped her. It snagged her shirt all the way down, which created a parachute effect. Sort of. It slowed her to a hundred miles per hour.

Back on her feet, she limped toward the bus stop across the street.

Because the Novaks lived in faux *Vyšehrad,* it would

follow that the neighborhood would be nice.

It wasn't nice.

No, it was a product of the devil. Those people out there needed Jesus.

A husband and wife argued on their front lawn, during their own garage sale, and the woman threw a hotdog at her husband. The man just sat there in his lawn chair, taking it.

Juliet could just imagine her father's response to such a thing.

Next the woman threw an entire package of hotdogs at him. Someone must've called the police at some point because sirens wailed in the distance.

"Should we intervene?" Juliet asked a portly fellow on the bus stop bench.

"What?" he asked, seemingly unaware of the scene unfolding behind them.

The bus arrived late and looked like it had spent seven years in the state penitentiary. And, it smelled like three fat guys in a two man tent.

Juliet huddled on a front seat with the collar of her leather coat pulled up around her neck. She put her leg up on the seat to dissuade others from joining her.

This is a survival situation.

The big guy with red hair didn't care. He almost sat on her leg.

Juliet was fast, though, dropped her foot, and squished herself against the side of the bus.

He grunted hello.

See, he's ... he's nice.

Dangling from his mouth was a toothpick. He didn't chew it. It just stuck there like he'd been in mid-pick, and then drifted off to another subject.

"Where are you going?" he asked, stuttering a little.

"Jinlin's Dine-In."

"That's a d-dump," he told her.

"Right? And the cook is an extortionist."

He nodded. "Sang Ook."

"Yesss!"

"He's the best of 'em." When he spoke, the toothpick jiggled. Any minute it'd drop off there and stick to something else.

Like on Juliet's Italian lambskin leather coat.

And I will die.

"W-watch out for W-ang Wei."

"Good, right. Good to know," Juliet told him, worrying about that toothpick more and more. So much so that she didn't realize that the bus had stopped.

"Are you going to g-get out?" the redheaded man asked, staring at her with dull green eyes.

Juliet stared out the window. Yumi's *Open* sign blinked on and off. Leaning left, she watched for a familiar serial killer, or the police, whichever.

The man stood and moved a step back so Juliet could squeeze by him.

Pushing herself forward, she kept her eyes on the parking lot.

"Y-you know what, this is m-m-my stop too," the redheaded man said. "Will you cross the parking lot with me?"

Juliet stared at him. Had he realized she was nervous? "Um, sure." Off the bus, she asked, "What's your name?"

"Louie," he said, lumbering behind her. "People at the bus stop call me Sc-screwy Louie."

Juliet frowned. "Why?"

He twirled one finger at his temple, indicating his mental status.

"Oh," Juliet said. "I – I'm sure that's not true."

"How about y-you buying me l-lunch?"

"What …? Yes. Yes, I will," Juliet told him and stepped onto the sidewalk in front of the Dine-In. "I'm meeting someone for lunch. Do you mind eating by yourself?"

He shrugged his beefy shoulders. He wasn't wearing a jacket. How had he managed the winter?

Juliet had two things in mind. Louie was hungry, and that was enough reason to buy him lunch, but she'd officially dubbed him her designated wingman. If a serial killer did come at her, maybe Louie could block the rope from getting around her neck.

Inside, the restaurant was already filling with customers. Juliet took a booth by one of the windows.

Louie took the booth behind her. He whispered, "What should I order?"

"Anything you want," she told him, watching the door.

Five minutes hadn't passed before a woman slipped into the seat opposite Juliet.

Portia!

Juliet sat straighter, wide-eyed. "Hi."

Portia's eyes were the same shade of green as Paris'. Her hair reached past her shoulders, but hers was coarser, curlier than her brother's. Maybe if Paris grew his out, it would look the same. Portia wore bangs, long ones that nearly covered her brows. She glanced across the room and then across the table. "Juliet?" Her voice cracked.

She was just as nervous as Juliet. She reached her hands across the table.

Portia took her hands. "Where is he?"

"He still hasn't shown up?"

"No," she said. Her green eyes had turned glassy, ready to cry.

"He's all right," Juliet told her, sounding more confident than she felt. Her heart thudded hard. "I'm sure he's fine. Paris is the smartest man I know."

Portia nodded. "He loves you too."

"Right," Juliet leaned back in the seat. "He's supposed to meet me here."

Portia adjusted her body so that she leaned on the table. "Let's just order some food and act normally."

"Right," Juliet said again and pulled a menu from the pocket on the wall beneath the window. "I don't think I can eat."

"I know," Portia said, nodding. She let out a long breath.

"Did Paris tell you that he spent his last dollar to portray an Amazon delivery guy?"

"No," she said, leaning forward. "So he's walking around in an Amazon uniform?"

It was going to be hard to get to know Portia at the moment. The girl held herself stiff, as though she was ready to bolt at any moment.

"He might've changed, but he has no money." She glanced toward the red lights on the ATM machine. "I want to give you both some cash." Juliet got to her feet and grabbed her purse from the seat. "Watch for him while I get some money for you and for Louie."

"Louie?"

"I'll tell you in a minute," she said and walked toward the ATM.

She'd just swiped her card when someone beside her

said, "Come back to give me more money?" He stood beside her with a cook's apron over his blue jeans and gray tee-shirt, which stank of seaweed and mutton.

Juliet gave him a smile. "No more money for you, Mr. Ook."

He bowed to her, just a little nod of his dark head, really.

"Did you use your money well?"

"I gave it to the poor."

She looked away from the cash machine for a second and stared at him. "Really?"

"No," he said with a teeter of a laugh. "I had casualties in a dice game."

"Then I will definitely not be giving you any more money," she told him. "I'll be doing you a favor."

He stood closer to her.

Juliet turned her shoulder. She'd been about to put in her pin number.

But Sang wasn't looking at her fingers but across the room. "You have new partner?"

Juliet glanced at the table toward Portia.

Portia had her head down, studying the cellphone in her hand. Had she heard from Paris? Was she on a burner phone?

Twisting back to the ATM, Juliet tapped the number pad. "I'm not giving her–or you–money."

"No, shouldn't bribe the police. Wind up in jail."

Juliet finished tapping numbers. "I wasn't going to bribe the po—" She turned toward him. "Why do you say that?"

He shrugged, facing Juliet again. "If you give that money to the woman at your table."

Juliet froze. "She's the police?"

"Yeah, she is the policewoman who was here when the lady died."

Her teeth locked down. Adams was behind this. He thought Juliet would tell the fake Portia where Paris was.

What if Paris comes inside?

Juliet finished the transaction and handed a hundred dollar bill to Sang. "Distract her."

"Yeah." He bowed again.

Juliet told him. "Give it to the poor."

He grinned. "They will be poor after I win tonight, yeah?"

Yeah.

Sang grabbed a platter from the kitchen window and moved toward the table.

The policewoman had spun around in the seat, maybe to watch Juliet in her peripheral vision. She was soon disabused of that notion.

Sang stood in front of her.

The woman stood.

The cook spilled a drink on her and then began screaming something in Korean.

It wasn't *Kung Pao Chicken.*

The policewoman looked down at her cute little dress…

Juliet walked fast toward the left, faked a right, and then skipped out into the alley.

As soon as she got outside, she worried about police cars: unmarked ones. Marked ones. There wasn't a vehicle in sight. Even the wheelchair had been removed.

She crossed the road and studied the woods. Was Paris in there, hiding out, waiting for the all-clear to enter the restaurant?

Juliet picked her way through the bloodroot and mayapple plants. "Paris?"

Everything was quiet. The scent of pine needles took over the smell of greasy duck, and the farther she walked, the stronger the pine smelled. "Paris?"

A pair of hands grabbed Juliet's arms and twisted her around. "Hello, my love," Paris said … and then he kissed her. Kissed her like he'd never done before with heat and passion until Juliet couldn't breathe. One arm went around her shoulder, the other around her waist.

He lifted his mouth. "I love you, Juliet. I love you."

She pushed his shoulders. "I love you too, but the police are here."

His brows jumped to his hairline. Holding Juliet firmly by the shoulders, he stared at her. "What did you say?"

"The police …"

"You said you love me."

Her cheeks heated. This was hardly the time to talk about it. Taking the money from her coat and shoved it into Paris' hand. "Go!"

But Paris wasn't listening. He pulled her to him again and kissed her as thoroughly as he'd done previously.

Juliet's heart nearly beat out of her chest, and for a few moments, she clung to him.

But panic soon took over. Pushing Paris away, she breathed hard. "Paris, run. The police are behind us."

"What?" he asked, a hurt look crossing his brow.

"Detective Adams has Portia," she said, her eyes hot as tears formed. "The police are inside the restaurant."

Paris' features fell. He released Juliet and stood back. "I'll find you," he said, reaching his hand toward hers. Then he turned and ran.

Juliet watched him, tears blurring her vision.

Paris weaved left around one tree and then turned toward another …

And then a colossal elbow came out from behind a tree and slugged Paris square on the jaw.

"Educated men are so impressive!"

Chapter 19

Paris' head jerked upward, and his body flew through the air for a couple of feet.

Juliet screamed and ran forward.

From behind the tree came a gigantic red-haired fellow. She skidded to a halt in the leaves. "Louie?"

"Sorry, Juliet," Louie said without stuttering. "I need to take Paris downtown."

How does he know my name…?

Juliet closed her eyes. "*Dios Mio!*" she said, bowing her head and flinging both her hands away.

Louie reached for Paris and pulled him up by the shirt

collar. Just with one arm, he managed it. "Come on, Buddy. Detective Adams wants to speak to you." From his back pocket, he pulled a zip-tie and cuffed Paris' hands.

Paris didn't fight him. He just stood there, limp, with blood gushing out of his nose and down into his beard.

Juliet started to cry. Storming forward, she shouted, "How could you, Louie? I will be disappointed in you every day for the rest of my life." And she was quite impassioned about it. "Plan on it. Every day you wake up, you remember that."

Louie's mouth turned down hard, and his voice held a note of concern when he said, "Well, that's just great. Thanks a lot. I probably will remember it now."

Suddenly there were a lot more people in the woods.

Fake Portia ran at Juliet, took her arm, and pulled her away from Louie and Paris.

Tires squealed into the alley, cruiser carriages scraped the ground. Lights flashed, but without sirens.

Five officers broke through the clearing, weapons drawn.

And then Detective Adams walked calmly into the clearing. He stopped in front of Paris first, gave him a once over, and then told Louie to put him in the car.

He turned around and eyed Juliet. "Your lipstick is smeared, Miss Da Vinci." And then he smiled as if he'd made a terrific joke.

On the one hand, what an asshat!

On the other, Juliet hadn't once thought that Louie was an undercover detective even though she knew the police were watching her, so really…

Who among us?

Adams took Juliet's arm. "Stay with me until we have

Mr. Nobleman in the car."

"He didn't kill anyone. You have no reason to arrest him."

It seemed he tried hard not to smile, but his lips did a weird thinning thing. "We'll start with evading police and go from there."

"Then, I'll go home …"

Adams didn't hold back this time. He laughed out loud. "Oh no, you're coming to the police station, just for a chat."

* * *

Juliet sat in an interview room for longer than an hour before someone spoke to her. She was sure it was on purpose. Would it kill them to put pictures on the walls and maybe a plant in the corner?

She'd draped her leather coat on the back of her chair, with the front pocket toward her.

Nicolo came into the room first and sat across the small table from Juliet. He didn't look her in the eye. Did she embarrass him? Did Nicolo cringe inside each time the lead detective interviewed her? He'd admitted it before: *You don't like Adams because he thinks faster than you.*

Nicolo wasn't dressed in his uniform, but in blue jeans and a pale blue knit polo that matched his eyes. His hair was loose and to his chin. Maybe he was undercover…

Dios Mio, was he at the Dine-In, and I didn't notice?

Someone turned the knob on the door really hard.

Juliet jumped.

So did Nicolo, but he tried to cover it by opening the manila folder he'd carried into the room.

Of course, it was Detective Adams making his big

entrance. He was just the sort of guy to use a door handle as a scare tactic. Did he imagine that Juliet was nervous or worried about the interview? He carried a manila folder too, and he slapped it hard on the wooden table before taking his seat.

Like that was his opening move: loud noises.

He grinned at Juliet and then sat in the chair next to Nicolo. He flicked his head, and his floppy brown hair swung out of his face. "Miss Da Vinci, we have a few questions for you."

"I've already answered your questions at tedious length. Let's get right down to the evidence."

Nicolo had his elbow on the table and rubbed his forehead with his hand.

Reaching into the pocket of her leather coat, Juliet pulled out the engagement ring and set it on the table.

Nicolo stopped rubbing his forehead.

Adams shrugged. "What is that?"

"You're not married?" Juliet asked. "It's an engagement ring."

"Did Paris propose?"

Oh look, wasn't the detective happy with his question. He turned his bright eyes on Nicolo.

But Nicolo didn't smile at all. His blue eyes flashed toward Juliet.

"It's Jana's engagement ring," she explained. "I found it in her bedroom."

"We checked her bedroom," Adams explained.

"You should've had your policewoman check the room."

A wrinkle appeared on the bridge of his nose. "So *you* found it in Jana's bedroom?"

"That's right." She stuck her hand into the coat pocket again and pulled out the badge, careful to keep her fingers on the edge. She set it on the table and carefully shoved it toward Adams with her fingernail.

He reached for it.

"Careful," she told him. "That's a master key to the rooms at the Porta di Messa. I found it between the seats of one of the vintage cars in Cyril Novak's garage."

The detective took a pencil from his pocket and, with the eraser, scooted it toward Nicolo. "Bag it." He turned his eyes on Juliet. With his forearms pressed to the table, he adjusted his weight in the chair. "Nobleman gave that to you, didn't he?"

"I just said I found it in the car at the Novak's house. You'll probably want to fingerprint the car. It's the 1961 Chevy Corvair, and it's green. It's the old car Mr. Yumi spoke about, and Sang Ook described."

Adams glanced at Nicolo. "Sang Ook … did we interview him?"

"I …" Nicolo pulled out the notebook from his shirt pocket and flipped through the pages. "I don't see a Sang Ook."

"He's a cook at the Jinlin's Dine-In," Juliet informed them. "He told me that an old green car sat in the alley before Jana was murdered. Whoever drove it was a blonde who smoked cigarettes." Leaning forward, she tapped her middle and ring fingers on the table to accentuate her points. "Someone in the Novak house turned off the security monitors at the house, borrowed the Corvair, and followed Jana. They accessed the balloon strings in the dumpster to strangle her. Bexley Pemberton-Kerr saw the entire incident because she had also stalked Jana to the restaurant. When she took off, the murderer followed her, and killed her too."

"The key was stolen to get into Pemberton's room," Adams said, nodding. "That's what the maid at the hotel thought, too. That's how she found Nobleman in the room."

"No," Juliet told him and shoved to her feet to pace the room.

Adams pushed back his chair and stood with hands on his hips, probably ready to tackle her if she made a move toward the door.

"We have to think," she told him, biting her thumbnail. "Paris did borrow a key, but not that one." She pointed to the bag in front of Nicolo. "That key was stolen earlier in the morning before the maid came to work." She lifted her gaze to Nicolo's. "Doesn't the coroner know when Bexley died? It had to be before Paris was in the room."

He looked at his notebook again.

Juliet paced again. "The killer got the key off the cart when it was still in the staff's closet. They borrowed a uniform, perhaps…" Juliet stopped pacing and spun toward the men. "What color are the uniforms at the Porta di…?

"You don't know?" Nicolo asked. "I'm surprised."

He needed to stop hanging out with Detective Adams so much. Nicolo was picking up the man's mannerisms…

"Red, white, and green," Juliet remembered.

Adams placed both his hands on the table. "So?"

She spun on him. "So, something green burned in the fireplace on the south side of the house the other day. Green tinted smoke drifted in the air."

"Muddying the waters …" he said and pushed off the table.

"I'm not muddying anything. Someone burned a vest in one of the fireplaces in the house. The dye in the vest turned the smoke green." She paced again. "So the killer borrowed a uniform, stole a badge, walked in and killed Bexley, and then ran." She paced the other direction. "They left via the fire escape without returning the uniform…" Juliet stopped and faced the men, eyes wide. "The bird show ticket."

Adams took a deep breath. "I'm afraid to ask."

Juliet reached for her leather coat. She'd worn it that day to the Porta di Messa hotel. Was the ticket still in her pocket? She checked one, and then another. There! She pulled out the cardboard ticket and put it on the table.

Adams glanced at Nicolo, wary, and then back to Juliet. "You're describing everything Paris did."

"Why would I do that? I'm trying to help him. Besides, Paris doesn't have a thing for birds."

Adams turned to Nicolo again. "I know she's trying to communicate with us."

Juliet dropped her shoulders. "I found that ticket in the fire exit stairwell … haven't you noticed all the birds in the Novak house? One of the Novaks was in the stairwell of the Porta di Messa."

"Just stop it," Adams let out, grabbing the evidence bags with the ring and badge inside. He told Nicolo, "I'm going to go get a warrant to search the car."

"But the birds …" Juliet said, stepping toward the table again.

"Tell Detective Montague if you must," he said with a weary tone and pulled open the door.

Nicolo kept his head bowed and got up from the table. He closed his manila folder before his blue eyes lifted and then narrowed in on Juliet. "Do you know how you sound?" His full mouth was set in a straight line.

Everything inside Juliet seemed to fall hard. Crashed. Her heart and her stomach hurt because of it.

"Yes, I sound crazy." She could stop her mouth from falling too. She pointed to the ticket on the table. "But, Nicolo, that zoo stub means something. I found it in the stairwell. The day after Bexley died. Hugo Novak loves birds, keeps dozens of them at the house."

He shook his head. "A ticket in the stairwell doesn't mean Hugo killed Jana and Bexley … and Noah. Why would he?"

She remembered Xenia's ideas. "Revenge, jealousy … mental instability."

He placed a hand on his hip. Lifting his chin, he looked down at her. "Motive?"

Juliet shook her head. "Jana was engaged to Noah, but broke it off. She wasn't wearing the ring, so she wasn't killed for it."

"Did Paris give you the ring?"

Her brows gathered. "No, he didn't."

"Okay," he said, holding up a palm.

"At first, we thought it was Noah, but he died … it all revolved around the engagement, I think. Someone didn't like it."

"We?"

Oh, he'd picked up on that, had he? Juliet didn't want to bring up Paris right then. "I'm using the royal *we*. You know, me, myself, and I…?" She shrugged. Then, "Anyway, I found the ring, I found the badge." She gazed at Nicolo again.

He hadn't dropped his fist from his hip.

"Someone's been following me, other than Screwy

Louie. They threw a wrench at me in the garage and broke into my room…"

Both of Nicolo's palms landed on the table, and he bent over it. "Why didn't you tell us?"

"There was no time. I needed to sneak out of the house and meet Paris."

His mouth formed a straight line, and he narrowed his eyes. "Don't you care at all what I think of you anymore? I know you still love me. Why would you throw things in my face like that? Paris, Paris, Paris."

"I'm in love with Paris," she said, not really believing that Nicolo would take it too badly. Nicolo didn't love her. Frankly, he didn't seem to like her much either.

But then again, maybe she was wrong.

Nicolo pushed off the table and stood very still. He wasn't demonstrative anyway, but this seemed different somehow. Were his insides crashing now?

Juliet's heart nearly stopped beating.

His mouth hadn't quite closed, and his eyes … they'd never lost their sparkle like this. "Are you serious?"

She whispered, holding his eyes. "Yes."

Right before her eyes, his complexion changed color, from a golden-hued to purple. His palm hit the table. "How could you?" His eyes sparkled again, this time in anger.

"I—I don't know," she said, not because Juliet didn't know why she loved Paris, but she didn't know how to answer Nicolo's question. "I'm completely committed to him, though."

His voice dropped. "You were completely committed to me not that long ago."

"Right," she said, "but you moved on."

Moving around the small table, he took Juliet's

shoulders and pulled her toward him. "I never moved on. Never. I was stupid and asked Roseline out, but I never cared about the girl."

She tried to step away, but his fingers tightened. "Nicolo," Juliet reasoned. "You don't even like me."

"What are you talking about?"

"I—You're always mad at me, disappointed in me, and you think I'm stupid."

"I think you're suggestible and jump headlong into situations that are very dangerous, and you scare me. But I love you."

He kissed her then, and his lips were warm and really lovely…

But Juliet's blood didn't warm. No tingling and yearning were happening. Pressing her fingers to his chest, she pulled away from him. "I'm sorry," she whispered. "I'm sorry, Nicolo. It's over."

He dropped his hands and took a step back. "All right." His voice was deep with emotion. "You're free to go."

"May I see Paris?"

"No," he said in a harsh tone. "No, absolutely not. He's being booked."

"Okay, then I'll go back to the Novaks, I guess."

"Do whatever you want," he told her without looking at her. Taking the file folder, he turned toward the door and flung it open. The door handle hit the wall with a loud bang and nearly slammed shut again.

Juliet grabbed it and watched as Nicolo walked away. Her stomach tightened, and her eyes burned.

* * *

An officer took Juliet back to the Blonde Palace.

She sat in the passenger seat without making a conversation. She couldn't speak even if the man had wanted to talk. Her throat hurt too because her heart resided there. It swelled so much that it blocked her air passages. Juliet could barely breathe.

She hated that she hurt Nicolo–didn't know she still *could* hurt him.

If he'd loved her all this time, why hadn't he said something to her? He'd never shown his love in any manner at all.

A tiny worm of anger slipped into her vacated chest. *How could I know?*

And if she had?

Juliet shrugged at the thought. It wouldn't have mattered. Paris had outshined the stars that Nicolo had flung into the sky of her heart.

How long had the officer waited before he said, "We're here" Juliet didn't know.

All she knew was that when she looked up, the cruiser was parked beneath the overhang at the front doors.

"Sorry," she told him, opening the car door. "Thank you for the ride."

House key out, she waved it in front of the badge reader and opened the door – and was entirely unprepared for what happened next.

Saskia stood at the bottom of the three marble steps, pointing her drink at Juliet. "See what the police dragged home?" She wore a gold lamé jumpsuit with her big hair hidden inside a lamé turban. She was Carman Miranda without the bananas.

Juliet's mother stood beside Saskia, dressed like

Saskia *still*, except her pantsuit was crushed copper sequins. Italia's hair was down and crinkly, and it had a few more streaks of blonde than the last time Juliet saw her. "Juliet, how could you?" She wore that *mother's face*. The one that was half disappointment and the other half was I-brought-you-into-this-world blah, blah.

"How could I…?"

"You brought that murderer into my house," Saskia said, giving Juliet a clue. "Hid him here."

Oh.

"Paris didn't murder anyone."

Saskia mounted the first step. "Then why did the police arrest him, you stupid girl?" Her stank attitude was actually in liquid form and she was trying to spray Juliet with it. "How dare you sneak around here? I opened my house to you."

Juliet glanced at her mother, hoping for a little support.

But, Italia had her head bowed in shame, as though she agreed with her beloved mentor and idol.

Nerves tingling so that her hand shook, Juliet repeated, "Paris Nobleman didn't kill anyone."

"Of course he did, you imbecile," Saskia said, her eyes running over Juliet. "He killed Jana and that other creature. He stood over her dead body. What don't you get? And, then, you bring him into this house…"

"No."

"He killed Noah. Do you approve of that? Obviously, you do. Are you the Bonnie to his Clyde?"

"*Baaastaaa!*"

The word reverberated in the wide-open space, bouncing off the chandeliers and the stairs and the bridges.

And it'd come from Italia!

Lifting her chin, Juliet's mother narrowed her amber-colored eyes and glared at Saskia. "Don't talk to my daughter like that you beefy-shouldered *maiala*."

Juliet's jaw dropped.

Saskia straightened to her full height. "Beefy…?"

That isn't the worst thing she just called you. Nope, huh-uh.

Italia took the first step on the foyer marble and lowered her head–like a bull ready to charge. She enunciated clearly, "Beefy."

Saskia's lip curled, creating a deep line around her mouth. "Get out."

"First-a you're gonna apologize to my daughter, eh?"

Juliet blinked hard. When had Italia morphed into Santos Da Vinci? And, was it only her imagination or had her mother developed a heavy Italian accent suddenly?

"Apologize?" Saskia said, glancing around the foyer. "I will never apologize. This is my house."

Italia lifted her brows and nodded, almost friendly with the expression. "You-a not gonna apologize? Is that what you said to me, is that what you said? To. Me?" Reaching down, she pulled off one high heel and held it over her shoulder. "Here's what we're gonna do…"

"Are you threatening me with my own shoe?"

Italia pointed it at Saskia's face and dropped her voice. "I'm not threatening you, *Minchione*. Apologize, or I'll kicka your ass." With her other hand, she pointed her index and pinky finger at Saskia and gave her the *malocchio*.

The evil eye!

Saskia turned toward Juliet. "I apologize for calling you stupid, Juliet. Please leave my house."

Italia dropped the shoe and stuck her foot into it. She also turned and looked at Juliet. "Go pack."

"Yes, *Matri*," Juliet said, heading for the stairs, feeling an immense sense of relief. She had her mother back. And, *Papa*, he had his wife again to keep his bed warm, eh?

On the first landing, she smelled cigarette smoke.

Cyril…

Juliet had her foot on the first step toward the third floor, but then changed directions. If Cyril was out here, smoking, then he wasn't in his office.

Were the security cameras still turned off?

She went to his office door. It was shut, and she tapped lightly on it. "Cyril?" When he didn't answer, she opened the door and peeped around the corner of it.

The room was empty. Cyril's computer screen was blank. Skirting the marble desk, she made for the closet and opened the door.

The system was back on, but there were no cameras relaying pictures of the room. In the center of the screen was a box, as for a password.

Biting her lip, Juliet adjusted the keyboard and typed in Czechia.

Nothing.

She tried again: *Vysehrad.*

Again, nothing.

Throwing all caution to the wind, she typed: IKilledEveryone!

The door to the office opened.

Juliet jumped away from the closet.

There was Cyril, smelling of smoke and regret. He was dressed differently than usual. No coat and tie today, but faded blue jeans and a pink polo shirt. His toupee sat crooked once more.

Taking a steady breath, Juliet said, "Sorry, I'm in your

office. I was looking for you … to say goodbye. My mother and I are leaving."

"Are you?" He'd paused at the door. "Well, I've just been showing several police officers to the garage. Thanks to you." He nodded, his fake hair moving with the action.

That rug don't love you, sir.

"You told them you found evidence of some sort and they're fingerprinting the Chevy. It'll be a mess." He shut the door and walked to the center of the room. "I'll need to have it professionally cleaned." His eyes went to his desk computer, and then drifted toward the closet. "Why is that screen up?" He moved around her.

Juliet followed him toward the closet. "Someone keeps turning off your screen."

"So you keep saying." He leaned forward to get closer to the screen. "You've typed a word."

"I did."

He turned on her, standing straight. "What are you up to?"

"I'm only trying to figure out who killed Jana … and Bexley, and Noah, too."

Cyril shrugged one shoulder. "That's what the police are for, young lady. They study at length to learn about clues and whatnot. You can't design a house without schooling, and you can't find a killer, either, without having a shiny badge on your pocket." He turned to the screen again and then pulled the keyboard closer to the edge. He typed in a word. It actually started with IK.

So, I'd been close…

Cyril straightened again and leaned toward the screen. "I want to know what they're doing in my car. They made me leave the garage." He nodded. "My own garage. The nerve."

"Seems as though they got here pretty quickly with a warrant. I only spoke to Detective Adams an hour ago."

He stared at the screen. "Yes, they gave us quite a scare when they showed up again. It felt like the day they told us about Jana."

That wasn't something Juliet had really thought about too much: the timing of everything that happened that day. Leaning against the desk, she asked, "What time of day did the police come … or was it the next day they told you Jana died."

He hit another key. "Um, I don't know, it was after lunch on the day she died."

Juliet brought her thumb to her lips and gnawed her cuticle. "Jana died at lunchtime."

Cyril glanced at her. "Yes, at that crappy little restaurant downtown."

The killer chased Bexley directly afterward…

That would've taken well over an hour, and then Bexley booked a hotel.

Whoever followed her waited until nightfall.

"The police came and took us into the parlor," Cyril told her, finally turning away from the screen.

Juliet pushed off the desk, her nerves humming. "Who was in the room when you found out?"

He stood in front of her then, frowning and thinking. "Hugo, Saskia, Mali … I think that's who was there."

She felt a little disappointed in Cyril's memory. He didn't pay much attention to things. "Teagan and Gerald weren't in the room?"

He stared out the window. "No, the police asked for the family to gather."

"What about Noah?"

"Oh, yes," Cyril told her, nodding, and making his toupee twitch. "Yes, yes, Noah was there. He took it rather quietly as I recall. He got up and left the room."

"So none of them could've been the murderer."

His eyes bulged. "What do you mean?"

"Whoever killed Jana killed Bexley Pemberton-Kerr in Mayville. That's a long drive. They wouldn't have made it back for the family meeting."

He shook his head. "I really think you ought to leave this to the police."

Juliet paced to the door and back to the desk. "Teagan wasn't there, neither was Gerald. Cammie overheard the conversation."

"Who's Cammie?"

"One of your," Juliet started, but then corrected herself. "I mean, one of your family's hairstylists."

"Well, I wonder why I've never met her," Cyril said, moving around the desk to sit in the chair there.

Oh, come on!

What would Cyril need with a hairstylist, other than purchase some hair plugs?

But, back to the puzzle. "Was Gerald around at all that day?"

"I don't remember," he answered, as though weary of the conversation.

Juliet stopped pacing and leaned her hip against the mahogany book cabinet. "What about Xenia?"

He spun in the chair. "What about Xenia?"

"Was she in the family meeting with the police officers?"

"Um …" Cyril leaned his head on the back of the chair and gazed at the chandelier. "I think … no, she wasn't there.

Okay, okay, now we have suspects.

Juliet put her hands on her knees and leaned forward. "Did you see Teagan later in the day?"

"I don't remember, honestly, Juliet. You're a dog with a bone, aren't you?"

"Cyril, did you just call me a dog?"

"With a bone, yes." He righted his chair.

"Fine. I'm a dog. Think this through for a second, who did you see later in the day? Who was mourning?"

He threw out his hand. "I don't know. I wasn't paying attention…" Then he sat up straighter. "You know what I do remember, though? It was the next morning. Very early. I didn't think anyone was awake."

"Right," Juliet encouraged.

"I went for a ciggy, you know? There was someone in the hallway. For some reason, the person changed directions when they saw me. I don't know if it was Gerald, but for some reason, I thought it was him."

"Where were you?"

"Down by the garage door."

Juliet stood and approached the desk. "Was the person blonde?"

"Yes, so I guess it wasn't Gerald. He looks like a lit match these days, doesn't he? But, he's always changing his hair color."

"He changes his hair color?"

Cyril shook his head. "You're asking me to remember a lot of things I'm not interested in, Juliet. Why don't you ask Saskia? She's always watching the boys."

"Right, I will," she told him, heading out the door. "Thank you, Cyril."

Juliet stepped out of the office and headed for the stairs again.

Her first intention was to go to the garage to tell Detective Adams what she'd learned from Cyril.

Or did Adams already know about the timing of it all? Surely, he knew who was in the meeting and who wasn't.

Hair color, hair color, why do I think something with hair…

Juliet stopped on the first stair step. She'd thought of hair color because she was pretty sure Gerald changed from blonde to redhead after he'd killed Jana and Bexley … because of the zoo ticket. What if he'd bought the bird show ticket for Hugo and dropped it in the stairwell while escaping Bexley's room after he'd killed her? He probably still wore the green service jacket he'd borrowed to blend in with other employees. He'd grabbed his regular clothes and trotted down the stairwell–and the ticket fell out without him noticing it.

When he came home, he asked Cammie to dye his hair. Then he'd pulled the vest from the car and burned it in Hugo's fireplace. That's why there was green smoke coming out of the chimney.

That means Gerald threw a wrench at me!

All the more reason to rat him out to the police.

Then, Gerald didn't like that Noah was getting so close to Hugo … so he pushed him over the railing with a noose around his neck.

Yes, yes…

Right?

There was one way to find out. She'd ask Cammie.

Taking the rest of the stairs to the bottom floor, Juliet wormed her way through the hallways behind the kitchen until she found the studio again.

Please be here, please be here.

But Cammie wasn't there. Actually, no one was inside

the studio. The lights were off at the stations. A gentle whoosh of air came through the vent, heating the space. The wood in the fireplace was dead.

Juliet remembered she'd seen a box in the trash near the styling station during her time with Cammie.

Would the box still be in the trash? How often was the waste taken out in a home salon?

Juliet looked into the first waste bin, next to the chair where Cammie had styled her hair. There was nothing in it, but one glance to the right showed a box of color still stuck out of the second bin. *Kerastase*, she remembered.

Juliet snatched it out of the bin and turned it around. If she were right, the color should be ruby grapefruit or some other name for the red color.

It was … *Caramel Ribbons*. Brown?

Something brushed Juliet's face and landed on her collarbone. She brought her hand up.

The rope around her neck pulled Juliet backward.

"Me thinks I see thee now, though art so low."

Chapter 20

The rope tightened.

Juliet's pulse skyrocketed, her heart nearly jumped out of her chest. She grabbed at the rope, tried to squeeze her fingers between it and her skin.

A black boot came across her stomach. A knee pressed against her chest.

Juliet's back hit the floor. She saw a black glove twisting the rope tighter … she gazed further upward, her breath cut off.

Xenia's face was a mask of fury, lips curled, her teeth bared. She yanked on the rope hard.

Juliet couldn't breathe. She swung her legs, kicked, and squirmed.

Xenia was on top, holding Juliet down.

Keeping one hand at the rope, Juliet raised her other hand above her head, praying for anything to hold on to, to pull herself away. Desperate, she swung her arm around.

Her hand landed on something metal, and she grabbed onto it. It was wrought iron…

Without knowing what it was, she fisted it and swung as hard as she could at Xenia's head.

The fire tool hit her, but Xenia fell sideways and then righted herself again. She held tight to the rope, hitting Juliet's head on the floor, choking her.

With what little strength she had left, Juliet raised the wrought iron poker again and belted Xenia's head. Not once, or even twice.

Many times.

Xenia fell to the side, her gloved hand raised to her temple.

Juliet rolled away from her. She held tight to the poker. Still, she could barely breathe. Her throat was on fire.

But she didn't have time to enjoy what breath she took in because Xenia got one foot on the floor and started to rise up again.

Juliet jammed the pointy end of the poker into the hardwood floor and pushed herself upward. Swaying a little, she drew the poker like a sword. Inspired by her mother's most recent insult, Juliet said, "If you think I won't stab you, you're wrong, you beefy-shouldered *maiala*."

Letting the loop end of the rope hit the floor, Xenia asked, "Who you calling a sow?"

Well, she got the general meaning, yeah?

Xenia tightened her grip on the end of the rope. "Where's the ring?"

"With the room key badge," Juliet told her, stepping to the left and toward the door. She tightened her grip on the end of the poker. "All safely tucked away."

"I'll find it, right after I kill you."

Juliet waved the poker at her. "My weapon beats your weapon."

Xenia opened one of the drawers on the stylist station and pulled out a hefty pair of long-bladed scissors. "I don't think so."

Okay, this is going to be harder…

Juliet eyed the distance to the door. It'd take a lot of breaths to reach it. She needed time to get her lungs back in shape. "Why'd you do it, Xenia? Why'd you kill them?"

Xenia was busy at first, admiring her new weapon. "He was mine first."

"Noah?"

"Yes, the little whore-man. He was never going to give any of them up."

Juliet adjusted her grip on the poker. Her hands sweated so much. "Why not just break up with him?"

"The mental illness thing we talked about, remember?" Xenia asked, shaking her head. "I'm on Sertraline. What are you taking?" And she said it so conversationally, too.

Juliet had never been so insulted in her life. "But why did you kill Jana? She'd broken up with him. I have the ring."

Xenia rolled her eyes. *Dios Mio*, what a bad attitude. "He'd talked her back into marrying him. He could talk anyone into anything."

Juliet gave her that one. "But, I have the ring."

"She hadn't put it back on yet. So, she died."

"And Bexley saw you…?"

"You know, that was my one mistake—don't you agree? I'd forgotten about her following everyone around."

Juliet nodded. "Who among us."

"Indeed." She took a step closer.

Acid spilled into Juliet's stomach. She went on, regardless. "Why didn't you kill Saskia then?"

"Wasn't it enough that I tampered with her Botox? I thought the poison would kill her. My second mistake, I guess."

"What about Teagan?" Juliet asked, her voice cracking a little. Her lungs were nearly back to full strength, but she'd had a slight hitch there.

"Teagan wasn't rich enough for Noah." She nodded. "Oh, he'd sleep with her, but he'd never marry her. That's why she wanted my nephew to marry her."

"Oh," Juliet said, nodding. "That makes more sense. And Mali?"

Xenia took another step.

Juliet stepped back one.

"See, that's why Noah had to die." She lifted the scissors and held them in her fist. "Where was it all going to end?" She ran toward Juliet.

Bug-eyed, Juliet swung at the scissors. She hit Xenia's arm.

Off-balance, Xenia brought the scissors down and missed Juliet's hand by a sliver of a hair.

Juliet swung upward and hit the woman's face.

It seemed to make Xenia very angry. She screamed in rage, and her face turned a purple color. Raising the scissors again, she jumped forward.

Juliet jumped too, sideways. She fell onto her side and skidded on the wooden floor.

Xenia followed her, kicking her in the legs and butt. She reached toward the floor and picked up the rope again. She swung it down on the poker, attempting to knock it away.

Juliet held onto it. She was on her back again, but she kept the poker with both hands and pointed it at Xenia.

Out of breath herself, Xenia just stood there. What was she doing? Thinking of her options?

Juliet kicked her feet and skidded away from Xenia. She got to her knees, weapon pointed.

Xenia lifted her chin. "I guess this was my third mistake."

And she turned and walked out of the studio.

Juliet stood there for a least a minute, pointing the weapon at the door.

Move.

Juliet took a step.

Move!

She slipped toward the door and gazed out into the hallway.

Heart pounding, she held the poker in front of her and ran. Toward the end of the hall, she spun around with the weapon out. Xenia could be hiding anywhere.

She got into the middle of the house before Juliet thought she might have a chance of surviving the ordeal.

Oh, how she wanted to live, just to kiss Paris again and to meet Amelia.

With no one popping out at her, Juliet ran hard toward the vintage garage and then burst through the glass door like a tornado, she and her fire poker. She kept the weapon up as she slid toward the police officers inspecting the Chevy Corvair.

Detective Adams saw her first. He held out the palm of his hand toward Juliet and stuck his other hand on the weapon at his waist. "Hold, hold, hold!"

Juliet dropped the poker, ready to fall to the floor too. "It's Xenia. She tried to kill me."

Adams shook his dark head. "What are you talking about now?"

Nicolo backed away from the Corvair. His blue eyes narrowed on her.

Juliet pushed her hair off the sides of her neck and revealed her throat. "Xenia Novak just tried to kill me in the hair studio. She ran away, I don't know where."

All five police officers stared at her with their mouths ajar.

Detective Adams was the first to regain his senses. With two fingers in the air, he directed his men. "We're looking for a white female, five foot eight or nine."

"Brown hair," Juliet added.

"Right, brown hair, and a boxy frame."

Juliet nodded. "And she's carrying long-bladed barbering scissors and a rope."

Every one of the officers pulled their weapons.

"Finnian, call for backup." Adams glanced at Juliet again. "You stay with me."

If he'd said that any other time, Juliet would've died a little inside. As it was, she was most happy to stay with Detective Adams.

The police swarmed the house.

Juliet stayed glued to Detective Adams. They remained on the ground floor near the French doors that led to the courtyard. The sun sank lower and lower, and the pool lights came on.

The Novaks remained in the kitchen while the house was searched.

Italia stayed right next to Juliet.

Adams had his hands in his pockets and watched the lawn.

And then it hit Juliet, and she said–louder than she'd meant to–"Birds."

"Oh, here we go again," Adams let out, his eyes rolling toward the ceiling.

"No," Juliet told him, opening one of the doors. Xenia has birds too, well, edible ones. She has a hen house. I'll bet that's where she's hiding."

Adams grabbed her arm, hard. "Where do you think you're going?" He stepped onto the patio and called to the men nearby. "This way," he told them.

Juliet followed, anyway. She stayed behind a large oak tree and watched them search the place through the window. It was chilly out, but the weather was changing. Warming.

"There," Adams said.

Juliet's stomach roiled. Had they found Xenia?

"Cut her down," Adams said.

Juliet repositioned herself and gazed harder to the left.

And, she recognized her–or at least she saw black boots and legs dangling in the air. Xenia had hung herself. At least she was consistent.

"My love as deep; the more I give to thee,
The more I have, for both are infinite."

Chapter 21

Juliet walked outside of the Erie Police Station with Paris. They were on the sidewalk, beneath a giant elm tree, where the afternoon sunlight sprinkled down on them. It was a warmer day, near sixty degrees. Juliet was back in her regular clothes, blue ankle pants, and a cream top and sweater.

Paris was finally out of his Amazon delivery man shirt and black slacks and into jeans and a sage green sweater that brought out the emerald of his eyes. His hair was already beginning to grow out from the shaved look. He was Juliet's Paris again.

Always Paris.

Juliet faced him. It was the first time she'd actually been alone with him since Xenia killed herself, and things had settled down.

Which was only yesterday.

She said, "Paris Nobleman?"

He'd stopped, his hands going to her waist. "Thank you for finding the killer. I knew I could count on you."

"Never mind that." She reached up, one hand in his hair, and pulled his face near hers. "I love you." Juliet kissed him, in front of the elm tree and the kids on the playground across the road.

Paris didn't take much persuasion, instantly returning the kiss, wrapping his arms around Juliet, and pulling her close.

Dios Mio, how had she ever stayed out of the man's arms?

But then Juliet remembered that she wanted to ask him something and pushed at his shoulders.

He wasn't going to give up so easily. Finally, he dragged his lips away, and in a ragged breath, said, "I love you, Juliet. Don't ever doubt it."

"Paris?" she asked, her stomach dancing all the way into her throat because she'd asked the question once before of someone with disastrous results. "Will you marry me–in a big way? You know, a huge wedding in the church with all of our family there, and Amelia right beside us?"

His green eyes widened. "Are you serious?"

Her stomach pickled even more. "Yes?"

And then he kissed her again, wildly and passionately. When he pulled his mouth away, he said into her hair. "As soon as possible, yeah?"

* * *

Three days later, Juliet met two ladies she'd been dying to meet for some time.

Portia waited on the steps of the children's home with a little girl in her arms.

Paris lifted Amelia into his arms while Juliet faced his sister.

Well, she didn't get a good look at the woman because they immediately embraced each other for over a minute. Portia said, "I'm so happy to meet you. I've heard about you non-stop since last summer."

Juliet held on tightly to her. Portia smelled of apple blossoms and honey. "I've been dying to meet you too."

Portia pulled away. "Almost literally, from what I understand." She was a gorgeous girl with wavy chestnut hair, full mouth, and green eyes. Her lashes were thick like Paris'.

And, then Juliet turned toward Paris and reached for the child. And, *Dios Mio*, what a beautiful girl. Skin like porcelain, chubby pink cheeks, and wild brown hair. Juliet knew how to tame that hair, oh yes. "Amelia, I love you already."

The child responded by grabbing a handful of Juliet's hair and pulling it into her mouth. Oh, those cupid bow lips, so like her father's.

Juliet told her, "I know, my hair is wonderfully amazing isn't it? But it's time to go. You need to meet your *Nonno and Nonna and to eat pasta, sì*?" She turned toward Paris' car already fitted with a baby seat.

Portia opened the driver's side door.

Paris nodded to Juliet. "Do you see how she morphs into her family?"

"She does eat, right?" Juliet asked, brushing the child's hair out of her face.

Paris nodded. "Bottles and mush."

Juliet shook her head and told Amelia, "That will all change now. *Bisnonna will feed you.*"

"Who's Bisnonna?" Paris asked, the sunshine touching his dark hair and turning it reddish.

"Tribly," Juliet told him. "She's a great-grandmother now. *Matri and Papa are Nonna and Nonno,*" she explained to Portia.

Portia screwed up her face and asked Paris, "Are you planning on moving in with the Da Vincis?"

Juliet answered, "Of course he is. Amelia needs all of her family under one roof. The room under the stairs will be her playroom."

"What about your new house?" Portia wanted to know.

Paris shrugged. "I thought you might want to live there. That way you'll be close to Amelia."

Juliet broke in, "Or you can live with my family. There's plenty of room."

"And the hot policeman you liked lives not too far away," Paris told his sister. He glanced at Juliet. "She found Nicolo Montague quite attractive."

Juliet gasped. "Nicolo and Portia? What a match." She waved her hand. "*Si,* I will arrange it."

Paris held the car door. "Totally morphed now. See what being a *matri does?*"

Juliet shook her head. "Oh no. I may be Amelia's mother now, but you will be my husband soon, and I will love you, Italian-style."

Paris straightened and took Amelia out of Juliet's arms. He said, "Put the baby in the car, will you, Portia?"

As soon as Portia lifted the child away, Paris took Juliet into his arms.

Thank you for taking the time to read *Thus With A Kiss*. I hope you enjoyed reading it as much as I loved writing it. Please consider telling your friends or posting a short review online. Word of mouth is an author's best friend and is much appreciated.

Thank you!

What's next from CJ Love?

CJ continues her Verona's Vineyard cozy mysteries with a trilogy featuring Delia from *O' Happy Dagger* and several of the other characters from the Juliet trilogy. Be sure to get your own personal notification of each new book by following CJ Love on Amazon or BookBub, and get all her exciting news each month by subscribing to her newsletter.

And if you love contemporary romantic comedy, check out CJ's hilarious *Wilde Girls* series.

Mysteries by CJ Love

Verona's Vineyard CozyMysteries Series
Juliet & Dead Romeo
O' Happy Dagger
Thus With a Kiss
Stage of Fools

Romantic Comedy by CJ Love
Lucy Goes Wilde
Wilde at Heart
Wilde Card

Historical Romance by CJ Love
For the Love of Murphy
For the Love of Lauralee
For the Love of Eileen (coming soon)

CJ Love authored four romance novels
before turning to the mystery genre. She started
writing when she was seven and didn't give up
until her books were accepted for publication.
Her quirky sense of humor comes through on
her website and her author pages at Amazon and
Goodreads. Nowadays, she writes full time from
her home in Largo, Florida.

Visit CJ Love's website at https://lovecj316.wixsite.
com/cjlove

And her blog at https://thatacus.wordpress.com/

**Sign up for her free mystery newsletter and receive
advance information about new books, along with a
chance at prizes, discounts and other mystery news!**

Contact by email: thiajwhitten@yahoo.com

Follow CJ Love on Twitter, Pinterest, Instagram and
Facebook